SILENT
PROTECTOR
VERONA BAY

Katie Reus

Cover art: Jaycee of Sweet 'N Spicy Designs
Editor: Julia Ganis
Author website: https://www.katiereus.com

Publisher's Note: This is a work of fiction. Names, characters, places, and incidents are either the products of the author's imagination or used fictitiously, and any resemblance to actual persons, living or dead, or business establishments, organizations or locales is completely coincidental.

Silent Protector/Katie Reus. -- 1st ed.
KR Press, LLC

ISBN-13: 9781635561845

For my mom.

Praise for the novels of Katie Reus

"Exciting in more ways than one, well-paced and smoothly written, I'd recommend *A Covert Affair* to any romantic suspense reader."
—Harlequin Junkie

"Sexy military romantic suspense." —USA Today

"I could not put this book down. . . . Let me be clear that I am not saying that this was a good book *for* a paranormal genre; it was an excellent romance read, *period.*" —All About Romance

"Reus strikes just the right balance of steamy sexual tension and nail-biting action....This romantic thriller reliably hits every note that fans of the genre will expect." —*Publishers Weekly*

"Prepare yourself for the start of a great new series! . . . I'm excited about reading more about this great group of characters."
—Fresh Fiction

"Wow! This powerful, passionate hero sizzles with sheer deliciousness. I loved every sexy twist of this fun & exhilarating tale. Katie Reus delivers!" —Carolyn Crane, RITA award winning author

"A sexy, well-crafted paranormal romance that succeeds with smart characters and creative world building."—Kirkus Reviews

"*Mating Instinct*'s romance is taut and passionate . . . Katie Reus's newest installment in her Moon Shifter series will leave readers breathless!"
—Stephanie Tyler, *New York Times* bestselling author

CHAPTER ONE

The sound of a ringtone pulled Adeline from the progress she was making on her painting. She'd been immersed in her work all day and had almost forgotten the thing.

Blinking, she turned, scanning the living room for the source of the noise. Seeing that it was Serenity, her business partner and best friend, she answered the phone. "Hey, what's up?"

"Just checking on you. Making sure you made it to the cabin safely." Serenity was using her mom voice now.

She grinned slightly as she sat on one of the leather couches of the lake cabin's living room. It was cushy, and with the rain pattering against the tin roof, she knew she could likely fall asleep with little effort. "I'm only about forty minutes away from you." She hadn't even left the state of Florida. But getting away like this was already therapeutic.

Adeline and Serenity had shut down the grooming side of their co-owned pet studio for a week since it was a quieter time of year for them. Christmas was a few weeks away, and while they kept the front portion of the shop open to sell dog treats and other pet accessories, both of them needed a break from the actual grooming part.

"I know, but you're there all alone."

Adeline appreciated that her friend cared enough to check on her—she loved having friends who actually cared. Not surface friendships, but the real deal.

Both of them had been through hell not long ago. Adeline had been kidnapped earlier in the year, though it felt like it'd been a decade ago. As if that part of her life was a far distant chapter in her past. Not that it was; she still occasionally had nightmares, still woke up covered in sweat at least once a week. "It's gorgeous here. Quiet, though it's been raining a lot today." She'd been hoping to get in some walks around the lake and to maybe test out the canoe in the boathouse, but instead had been holed up with the fire going and painting...almost all day, she realized when she saw the time. Her stomach rumbled, reminding her that she hadn't eaten since breakfast. And coffee didn't exactly count.

"I'm glad you're getting some downtime."

"How's *your* downtime?" Adeline wasn't sure Serenity actually got any. Her friend was a busy mom who seemed to have a hard time saying no to people.

"Harper gets out of school next week so I'm catching up with Christmas shopping, wrapping presents I've hidden, and all sorts of other things now that I have free time."

"I hope you're sneaking in extra alone time with that sexy man of yours?" Serenity's fiancé Lucas—soon-to-be husband—owned a local construction company and was just as busy.

Serenity snickered at that. "Maybe."

"Good. You guys deserve it." And lord knew Adeline wasn't getting any lately. It had been so long for her that she didn't even want to think about the actual time frame, much less say it out loud. So she hoped her friend was making up for her lack of a sex life.

"Tell me exactly how glorious it is being all alone," Serenity said, a slight note of wistfulness in her voice. "I love my family, but I'm kind of jealous."

"Well, I'm about to take a hot bath, pour some wine, and curl up by the fire with a book. So bring on the jealousy."

Serenity groaned slightly and then there were voices in the background, very likely Harper and Lucas. "I've got to go. I just really wanted to make sure you were doing okay. Keep the phone lines open—don't completely hole up this week."

"Okay."

After they disconnected, she sat there for a long moment. She knew Serenity worried about her, but for the most part she was handling the aftereffects of her kidnapping okay. Except when she glanced down at the faded burn marks on her left arm, a reminder that she had almost died. *Again.* Though Serenity didn't know about the time before. Didn't know about her other scars.

No one in Verona Bay did.

Her gaze strayed back to her painting and she stared at the almost-finished canvas for a long moment. She hadn't even meant to paint her mother, but once she'd started, there had been no stopping her. She'd been consumed with thoughts of the past, and now...looking into the dark eyes of her deceased mom, she wondered what her mom would think of her. Would she be proud? Sighing at herself, she grabbed her paintbrushes and took them to the kitchen sink to wash everything out.

A friend from Verona Bay had let her use this cabin for the week, saying that since it wasn't rental season, she was just glad the place was getting some use. The woman wasn't charging Adeline rent or anything, though Adeline was going to give her something to cover the stay.

The cabin was on a fairly large lake, but not so large she couldn't see the other side. Though there were no direct neighbors, she still had a view of the huge homes dotted around the lake. And she had phone and internet access out here. But it was nice not to have to deal with other humans close by. Sort of a way to decompress.

After pouring herself a glass of wine, she did exactly as she said she would: started a hot bath and pinned her hair up on top of her head before sinking into the water.

This was her vacation and she was going to take full advantage of it.

* * *

Mac frowned as he pulled into the driveway. Fresh tire tracks led to the closed garage. Derek had told him he could use this lake house to get away for a few days. God knew he needed it.

His brother Joe had invited his girlfriend over for the last few nights, and while he'd never minded living with his two younger brothers, lately Mac was starting to crave some space. To carve out something just for himself. But he didn't want to kick them out or anything. After their parents had died, Mac had finished raising Joe and Dylan. They all still lived in the house they'd grown up in. He couldn't very well tell his brother he couldn't bring his girlfriend around. It was just weird having an outsider in his space so often.

And if he was being honest, seeing them together reminded Mac that he'd somehow blown his shot with Adeline Rodriguez. He wasn't sure how, but at one point there had definitely been a spark of attraction between them. Hell, more than a spark. The simmering heat between them had been electric.

But the moment he'd asked her out, she'd pulled back as if he'd asked her to make an animal sacrifice with him. And for the last two months she'd basically been avoiding him.

No matter how hard he tried, he couldn't get her out of his head. It was because he knew he hadn't imagined the spark between them, the pull. She'd felt it too, and he knew she was single. But something was keeping her away from him.

Sighing at himself, he grabbed his duffel, and, bracing for the deluge of rain, hurried out into the weather. He raced for the front door, then, using the key Derek had given him, let himself in.

He froze for a moment, carefully setting the bag on the floor as water dripped down his face and arms. He was *not* alone.

Music drifted from somewhere inside and he heard definite movements above the rain pattering against the roof. He knew Derek rented this place out in the summer, but not the fall and winter. Derek had also told him the alarm would be active but... Mac glanced at the panel by the front door. Nope, it was disarmed.

He stepped cautiously through the foyer, his muscles tensing as he prepared to deal with an intruder.

Moving down the hallway, he heard a soft humming, and a sort of sizzling sound. And...a deluge of spices, something delicious, hit him. Someone was cooking in the kitchen? So the intruder was just making themself right at home.

As he stepped around the corner, he froze at the sight in front of him.

Adeline was in the kitchen, wearing a skimpy little...dress? Lingerie? He didn't know what the scrap of material was, but she wore it well. The pink dress thing had skinny straps, the color bright against her darker skin, and showed off the most perfect ass he'd ever seen. And she was humming to herself as soft music played and she swayed her hips in the most sensual, free way he'd ever seen.

Oh, hell. He felt like he was the intruder, knew he needed to let her know he was here. "Adeline."

She let out a scream and whirled to face him, spatula held up like a weapon. Then she froze. "Mac? What...are you doing here?" She blinked those big brown eyes at him.

"Derek told me I could use this place for the next two days."

She winced and let out a nervous laugh. "Ah, well, Madison told me I could use it."

Derek's wife. "They clearly made a scheduling error." Though he was disappointed to have to leave, he took a step back. "I'll get out of your hair." Seeing her jarred him, especially since he'd been more or less obsessing about her the last couple months. Hoping for little peeks of her around town even though it was torture of the best kind. And now she was standing in front of him, her breasts spilling out of the dress, his fantasy come to life.

She shook her head slightly, her big curls swishing softly against her shoulders. "No, it's late, and the weather is awful."

"It's only nine o'clock."

"The rain..." She trailed off and then looked down as if suddenly realizing what she was wearing, because she cleared her throat. "Ah, hold on." She turned off the stovetop and hurried from the room.

When she did, he got a glimpse of a lot of skin and a hint of her ass as the little dress thingy flared out.

His muscles seized up as his awareness of her heightened. He'd always been attracted to her. From the moment she'd shown up to tutor one of his brothers. But damn, seeing her like this? He scrubbed a hand over his face and tried to shake away the lust surging through him.

Less than a minute later she was back, wearing a big sweater with a sparkly heart in the middle and yoga pants. "We should probably call Derek and Madison and find out what happened. Or at least let them know."

"I promise, it's not a big deal. I'll just head out." He hadn't even gotten settled in, though he was disappointed. He'd been looking forward to the time alone here.

A boom of thunder clapped overhead and they both stilled for a moment as the windows rattled.

She shook her head as she returned to the stove. "The rain is getting worse and I just got a tornado alert on my phone." As if to mirror her words, his own phone buzzed with the standard alert, announcing that a tornado had been seen in the area. "You shouldn't be on the roads with this weather. There are probably trees down too." She spoke as if it was already a done deal.

She was right, he knew that. But he didn't want to invade her space when she'd made it clear that she didn't want to be around him. He glanced around the kitchen, studiously *not* staring at her. "Smells good."

"It is good, and I've got plenty to share. Seriously, there are two bedrooms. Go put your bag in the spare one. It's the first one on the right down the hall. I took the bigger bedroom." She grinned slightly and that smile did something to his insides—namely, made him forget how to breathe. "To be fair, I didn't know you were coming."

The situation was so weird and she was being so *nice* to him. As if she hadn't been avoiding him for months. And...he really didn't want to drive home. Not because of the storm, but because he wanted to spend time with her.

In that moment, he decided he wasn't going to look a gift horse in the mouth. He simply nodded and back-tracked to the foyer, grabbing his duffel and doing as she said.

As he stepped into the spare bedroom, thunder shook the entire house and he figured they might need to get some candles in case they lost power. He texted Derek to let him know about the double-booking and to ask where the emergency kit was.

Mac couldn't shake the surreal feeling as he stepped back into the kitchen to find Adeline scooping whatever she'd cooked into two white scalloped bowls.

"I'm going to top mine with a fried egg. You want one?" she asked.

He glanced at the bowl of rice and beans and looked up at the sliced avocado on the cutting board. "Yeah, thank you. This looks delicious. What is it?"

"A modified version of my mom's huevos rancheros—I don't include the corn tortilla and I don't make my own salsa." She laughed lightly, the sound wrapping around him. "I use the store-bought kind," she said as if confessing a secret. "My mom used to make this for me all the time. I've never quite perfected the spices she used on the rice, but it's pretty close."

"She used to?"

"Yeah, she died." She didn't look at him, didn't offer up any more details, but he saw the way her jaw flexed slightly as she cracked an egg into the pan.

Mac recognized the sharp bite of pain in her words, something he understood all too well, having lost both his parents at a relatively young age. So he didn't push.

Before he could think of something to say, she continued. "I've got an open bottle of wine over there. I'm not sure if you drink wine, but you're welcome to have some. And there are a couple beers in the fridge. Derek's, I'm sure."

He shook his head as he stepped farther into the kitchen. "I don't drink at all, so I'm good."

She paused and glanced over at him. "You don't drink alcohol?"

"Nope."

"Well, I've got water and tea in the fridge."

"I've got a cooler out in my Bronco. I wasn't going to haul it in until the morning." He'd planned to get here and crash.

"Did you eat before leaving Verona Bay?"

He laughed lightly as he leaned against a countertop. "Does gas station beef jerky count?"

She looked at him again, her brown eyes widening in horror. "No, it most certainly does not."

Being this close to her was doing something to his senses—namely sending them into overload.

Pushing up, he searched around for silverware and set the little table by the window overlooking the lake. The blinds were open but it was too dark out to see much. If he squinted, he could just make out the lake beyond the sheets of rain falling.

"The flashes of lightning are kind of wild. They've been lighting up the lake. It's cool to see," she said.

He turned away from the window. "I texted Derek and let him know about the mishap. I also told him about the thunderstorm. He told me where all the spare candles are, so I'll grab them and set them up."

"Good idea, because I didn't even think of that… Do you mind if I drink, by the way? If it'll bother you, I don't mind putting the wine up."

He was momentarily stunned by her intuitiveness but maybe he shouldn't have been. Most people didn't catch on to what he meant when he said he didn't drink at all. He always said it so matter-of-factly. Usually people just thought he meant he wasn't drinking right then. "No, I'm good, I promise. I'll be right back."

He stepped into the laundry room and found the box of battery-operated candles, regular candles, flashlights, little tea lights and other assorted things that made up the equivalent of a hurricane kit and carried it back to the kitchen. He set everything on one of the countertops as Adeline set both their bowls on the table.

"I'm sorry to disturb your getaway," he said as he joined her in the eating nook.

She snorted softly and motioned for him to sit as she took her own seat. "I could say the same thing. You're obviously up here to get away too. Sorry I ruined that for you."

"Being around you is a nice change of pace. I haven't seen much of you the last couple months." Damn it, he hadn't meant to say anything. He didn't want to make things awkward, because it was clear she was trying to keep things light and upbeat. Apparently he couldn't help himself.

It definitely wasn't his imagination when her cheeks flushed.

He cleared his throat. "Sorry, I wasn't trying to make it awkward. You're just being really nice to me. It...surprised me since it feels like you've been avoiding me."

"No, it's fine. I guess...I have *maybe* been avoiding you."

"Maybe?"

"Fine, I have been." Her cheeks flushed even darker and she avoided looking at him as she picked up her fork.

"Just because you don't want to go out with me doesn't mean we can't be friendly." It bothered him that once he'd asked her out, she'd basically ghosted him.

"It's not that I didn't want to go out with you... I did. I do. I mean..." Her cheeks were flaming now. "I don't even know what I'm trying to say. I'm just not dating right now and I guess I panicked. I didn't want things to be weird, so I flaked."

He focused in on the "I do" statement. Interesting. He wasn't sure what to think about it.

"So how was the drive up here?" she continued, clearly trying to change the subject.

He took her up on it, not wanting things to spiral into a weird place, especially when they were currently sharing a roof. "Not too bad until the rain started. The roads were getting slick the last couple miles here. And the lightning—" As if on cue, lightning flashed across the sky, highlighting the lake in brilliant streaks of white.

Across the table, she shuddered slightly.

Protectiveness surged through him. He didn't like it when anyone was afraid, but especially not Adeline. Not after what she'd been through. "After we eat, we might want to set up some of the candles just to get things ready." He glanced over at the fireplace. "And I can get that going again."

"Yeah, I kind of let that fall by the wayside. I took a bath and then got distracted with cooking."

The vision of her naked in a tub wasn't making the attraction dissipate any. Nope. Not at all. "This is amazing, by the way. I think your mom would be proud." He took another bite, ordering himself not to shovel it all in like a barbarian.

"Thanks." Her cheeks flushed again and he had all sorts of thoughts about that—namely wondering if she'd flush all over if he had his head between her legs.

Silence stretched between them and he couldn't decide if it was comfortable or awkward. Things between them were weird but she'd admitted that she'd been avoiding him and...being here with her didn't feel off. He liked her company, liked *her*, and she was trying to make the best of things.

"Can I ask why you don't drink?" she asked suddenly. Then her eyes widened slightly. "I mean, never mind, I'm being really nosy. When I'm nervous I tend to talk too much and say stupid stuff. Just ignore me."

His mouth curved up as he watched her. He'd never seen her out of sorts like this. She was sweet and funny—always making his brother laugh when she tutored him. But out of sorts? No, definitely not.

"It's okay. I don't mind talking about it. I've been in AA for about thirteen years. I don't have the urge to drink anymore." He paused. "Actually, I should say I get the urge maybe once a year, but it usually passes. I'll wonder if now I can have just one drink and be done with it. But I'm simply one of those people who can't drink. I just don't know when to stop. It's like there's a switch in my brain that doesn't shut off. In high school it wasn't a big deal, and in case you haven't heard, I had quite the reputation as a partier."

She nodded. "I've heard some stories."

Yeah, he figured, and hoped she hadn't heard the worst ones. He'd been young and stupid, but it was still embarrassing to think of the way he'd been. "So anyway, that was normal, or I thought it was. I was young and stupid and all my friends were doing it." Of course his friends hadn't been drinking on weekdays after school like he had been. "In the Marines I basically got my shit together. When I was deployed, I wasn't drinking much except if we managed to sneak some into our tents. But it soon became clear that unlike my friends, I simply couldn't stop. One of my superiors had a long sit-down with me about what my life would be like if I didn't get it together, and I looked into AA, got a sponsor and got that part of my life together.

"It's not as simple as all that—I hurt people in ways I regret, had setbacks, and I screwed up more times than I want to admit—but that's the short story of the long road I took to get here. It's just part of who I am, and I'm at the point now where it's something I manage." He didn't hide this part of himself, but he also didn't normally talk so freely about it. But he liked being open with her, wanted her to know exactly who he was. Especially since he thought there might still be a chance between them.

"You still go to meetings?"

"Once a week. It's healthy for me to connect with others, remind myself that I can't *ever* risk going back to who I was." He'd built up his business, had two brothers to look out for, and he *liked* his life. Ruining everything over a temporary numbing wasn't worth it.

She took a bite of her dinner, nodded thoughtfully. "My mom was an alcoholic. I've always been cautious about how much I drink because of it. I know it can be hereditary."

"My dad was one too. He covered it well, but knowing what I know now, yeah, he had a problem. I just didn't see it when I was a self-involved teenager. I honestly don't think he realized he had a problem. It was sort of the culture of him and his friends, I guess." He cleared his throat. "Can I ask you something personal?"

"Yeah, of course, especially after you've been so open." She watched him with those gorgeous brown eyes he could lose himself in.

"You never talk much about your past. I guess I don't have a question, I'm just curious, and now you've brought up your mom, so..." Hell, he didn't know what he was trying to say. He just wanted to get to know her more.

"Ah, well, my mom...she was an artist. A talented one. Drinking and drugs were very much part of her and her artist friends' way of life. She certainly didn't think she had a problem, never would have labeled her drinking alcoholism, but...she drank to the point where it was unhealthy."

Before he could say anything else, another bolt of lightning streaked across the sky, lighting up the lake again right before the cabin plunged into darkness.

CHAPTER TWO

Adeline jumped when the lights suddenly blinked out, then went very still. It was so dark—the kind where you could barely see your own hand in front of your face. "Mac?" she whispered even though she knew he hadn't gone far. It was just so quiet.

"Just sit tight. I'm going to turn on some of the candles."

His deep voice was calming as his chair scraped back against the wood floor. Then another flash of lightning lit up the room as he moved across the kitchen to where he'd left the box of supplies. She shivered as they were plunged back into darkness again and found herself very happy he was here. The thought of being alone right now, in a remote lake cabin without power? Under the best of circumstances she wouldn't be okay with that, but after the year she'd had... No thanks. After being kidnapped, she'd woken up disoriented and at night in that shitty FEMA trailer. There had been no light. Being in the dark was still disorienting. It was why she now slept with a night-light.

Still, Mac showing up unexpectedly had her off-kilter in the worst way possible. She felt like a mess, just blurting stuff out. And having a slight buzz from her wine likely wasn't helping either. But around Mac Collins she tended to speak before she could think things through. It had been like that from the moment she'd met him near the beginning of the year.

She'd shown up to tutor his younger brother and been sort of awestruck by the big, sexy man. Good God, he was what fantasies were made of. Tall, broad shoulders, ridiculously muscular arms and a beard that gave him that dark, brooding lumberjack look—which was only helped by the flannel he wore in his woodworking shop. And those electric blue eyes were like icing on the cake of sexy Mac Collins. Well, maybe his forearms were the icing—those she would definitely like to lick. His forearm game was no joke.

And oh God, she had to stop spiraling over him.

Little lights flickered on suddenly and she saw that Mac had gotten a couple of the battery-powered candles turned on.

She let out a breath she hadn't realized she'd been holding and it came out in a loud whoosh of noise.

"You okay?" His deep, rumbly voice sent a shiver of awareness through her.

"I'm good." Just embarrassed by her fear of the dark. Now that the little lights were on, and she could see him a mere ten feet away in the kitchen, it made her feel more grounded, knowing they wouldn't be stuck in utter darkness again. Carefully, she pushed up from the table, leaving her wineglass and bowl where they were.

Another line of lights flickered on across the countertop, and as she reached him, Mac handed her a flashlight.

"It's got a short lanyard on it. You can keep it hooked around your neck so you'll never be—"

The lights suddenly shot back on and she sucked in a breath for a whole different reason. Being this close to Mac under the bright intensity of the kitchen lights was a whole lot of Mac goodness. He smelled earthy, sexy, and yep, she had to stop the mental spiral that seemed to happen around him. She thought of it as "the Mac spell."

His gaze fell to her mouth and heat bloomed in her middle, spilling out, lower, lower.

Ooohhh, no. Clearing her throat, she took a small step back. This really wasn't a good idea. Her track record with men was what horror movies were made of, and she refused to allow herself to do something dumb just because they were alone and she'd had too much wine.

Except…she'd only had a couple glasses. And she knew what she wanted, with wine or without.

Mac.

She'd wanted him since she'd met him, had fantasized about his big hands and full mouth far too often. She'd resisted the urge to paint him—so far—because it felt almost intrusive, but the urge to capture his face on canvas was there.

He took a step away as he pulled out more candles and she could breathe again. "Let's go ahead and set these up in the living room, kitchen, the bathroom and bedrooms. Might as well get them going because we'll lose power again, I'm sure."

It was a relief to have something to do to keep her occupied, to keep from obsessing over his gorgeous, kissable lips. "Okay, and I'll go ahead and load up the dishwasher while we've still got power. Clean everything up while we can."

"Sounds good. I'll start with the living room and get the fire going too."

They moved into action and she was glad to have something to do with her hands—something that kept her mind from wondering what was under Mac's shirt.

* * *

Adeline settled on the couch as Mac finished stoking the fire. Being here with him was bizarre but he'd ended up being a good person to have with her during a crisis. Not that having the power go out was a real crisis, but he was so unruffled about everything. A solid rock. In more ways than one.

"So, how's work?" She needed to keep things in neutral territory and wasn't quite ready to go to bed yet. So even though being around him had her senses going haywire, she wanted to spend more time with him. He made her feel safe, and work was safe enough territory.

"Good. Exhausting, but I love what I do. So no complaints." He did custom woodwork, whether it was furniture or pieces of art, and the man was insanely talented. There was a long-ass waiting list for him and she was pretty sure he had jobs scheduled for the next two years. His customer base was worldwide and didn't mind waiting. He also did custom projects for a local construction company—owned by her best friend's soon-to-be husband.

"So you just decided to get away in the middle of the week?" She picked up her mug of hot tea, having switched over to it once they'd cleaned everything up and set up all the candles. The power was back on but they'd turned off most of the lights anyway, letting the fire illuminate the living room. The crackling and soft heat made everything feel cozy, intimate, as if the outside world didn't exist at all.

"Joe's been bringing his girlfriend over a lot lately." Mac's tone was dry as he sat in one of the comfortable chairs by the fireplace, angling himself toward her.

"You don't like her?" Adeline had met Marcy before, and when Joe had been missing, the woman had been distraught.

"No, she's nice. She's good for him. It's just... There are a lot of people in our house all the time now. It's been an adjustment for me."

"I bet."

He seemed like he was more or less a loner. Or maybe not, because he was tight with his brothers. But he looked after them and was more of a fatherly figure than a brotherly one. She guessed it was an adjustment because his brothers were now adults with their own lives, not teenagers who needed tons of guidance.

"So look, I'll head out of here tomorrow and you can stay," she said. She had a house to herself and didn't mind heading back home. It was clear he needed space and she wanted him to get it.

"No way. I'll head out in the morning." Thunder crashed overhead then and they both glanced out the window as a jagged bolt of lightning streaked across the sky.

It was gorgeous and a little terrifying at the same time. A type of art all in itself.

"Or maybe not," he murmured. "We'll see what happens with the weather. Did you paint that?" He nodded toward the painting she'd left in the corner.

She wasn't done, still needed to do some finishing touches and fix some of the shading, but it was really coming into focus now. "Yeah."

"You're really talented. I didn't realize you painted like this." There was a touch of awe in his voice, which for some reason made her all warm and fuzzy inside. "The woman is stunning."

She felt her cheeks heat up and tried to shrug off the compliment. "It's my mom." And she *had* been stunningly gorgeous. Adeline had managed to capture the faint auburn streaks in her mom's dark hair that had only been visible in the right light, the intensity of her dark eyes and the smile. The big, infectious one that had made many men and women offer her the world. In the background she'd barely sketched in a few sailboats on a lake, the little marks more abstract than anything. The painting had evolved from a long-buried memory, one where it had been just her and her mom spending a day together. They'd had a picnic and some guy had offered to take them sailing—but her mom had said no, blown him off so she could spend the day with her daughter. She'd •

chosen Adeline that day, something she hadn't always done. "But compared to her talent, this is more like a finger painting." Okay, that was an exaggeration, but it felt weird to be complimented on painting when that had always been her mom's thing.

He snorted softly. "Somehow I doubt that. Do you sell your work?"

"No. Painting is something I do for me. It's a creative outlet. I've thought about it, but it's not something I want to monetize. Not yet anyway. Who knows what the future holds though." When she'd settled in Verona Bay, she'd wanted to slough off all aspects of her past. Though lately she'd toyed around with the idea of opening an online shop. She tutored math on the side to make extra money, and loved it. She was afraid that if she turned painting into a way to make money, she'd lose the joy of it.

"Yeah, that's why I like to fish. It gets me out of the shop, into nature and away from everything." He looked at the painting again and that same awe lit up his blue eyes. "Though to be fair, I couldn't make any money from fishing. You, on the other hand, could probably make bank."

She didn't show most people her paintings, and he was so sincere in his compliment. She cleared her throat, feeling even more out of sorts. "How's Joe doing after everything?"

"That kid bounced back so fast. He's fine." Mac snorted as he shook his head. "You'd never know he almost died and was floating out in the waterways for days."

She shook her head, tension banding around her chest as she remembered what he'd looked like when they'd found him on the river. Joe was about a decade younger than her, but sometimes it felt like more than age separated her and Joe. He was a goofy, funny college-age kid who had a good attitude about everything. She wasn't surprised he was doing well.

"So at the risk of making this awkward, can I ask you something?"

She tensed slightly, but nodded. "Yeah."

"I know I didn't imagine the chemistry between us. Why did you say no when I asked you out?"

Technically Adeline hadn't said no, she just hadn't answered and then they'd been interrupted. Aaaand then she'd ignored him for months like a coward. Even though her instinct was to curl in on herself, she kept her gaze on his. "My track record with dating isn't awesome."

"So...you're just never going to date again?" He stretched out in the chair, his long, muscular legs a feast for the eyes.

Her gaze flicked to his thighs, paused, and she had to lock down her thoughts because they were straying into very dangerous territory. "I didn't say that."

"Well, are you dating? I don't think I've ever seen you out with anyone." His voice was all rumbly, deep, and gah, why did she like it so much?

"I've never seen you out with anyone either." It wasn't exactly a question, but she was curious. Soooooo very curious. And maybe even a little jealous.

His mouth curved up slightly. "Fair enough. I haven't dated in a while either. Longer than I want to think about. Since moving back home, taking care of my brothers, getting my business off the ground... Dating didn't really factor into anything."

Yet he'd asked her out.

As if he'd read her mind, he continued. "Until you, dating wasn't on my radar. And at the risk of sounding pathetic, if you ever want to go out, the offer is open. I would love to take you to dinner."

Oooooh. She felt the heat of his look all the way to her core. And that look said he would like to do more than simply take her to dinner.

She shifted slightly in her seat, the warmth in her cheeks having nothing to do with the crackling fire or hot tea. She wasn't sure how to respond even though she really, really wanted to take him up on his offer. "Ah, okay."

But fear had dug its way into her chest, sinking in razor-sharp talons. She might have started over in Verona Bay, made a life and friends, but she'd never opened herself up to anyone in...a really, *really* embarrassingly long time. For good reason.

The last man she'd been in a relationship with was dead. Because she'd killed him.

CHAPTER THREE

"Pretty sure we're lost." Marcy's tone was skeptical as they trekked down the nature trail.

"No, I know this area." Maybe if Joe sounded confident, she'd believe him. Joe looked around at the woods on either side of them, fighting a frown as the misty rain covered their faces and jackets. Behind his family's property were miles and miles of trails. Long before he'd been born, his parents had bought thirty acres and never developed the land other than to build a house and create trails for him and his brothers.

The rain had finally cleared up this morning so he and Marcy had decided to take a hike behind his family's property. They'd only been out for thirty minutes when the bottom of the sky had fallen out again. They'd tried to keep going, but had ended up going off trail and had hunkered down under a cluster of trees in an attempt to stay dry.

Once the rain had eased up, Joe had been turned around. He didn't come out here that often, usually only with his oldest brother Mac—and only because he wanted to hang out with Mac, who loved the woods. Joe preferred gaming, taking his boat out, and indoor rock climbing. But Marcy had wanted to go hiking, and now... Hell, they were lost.

"Really?" Doubt laced her voice, and when he looked back at her he saw the annoyance flickering in her pretty green eyes. Even with her polka dot raincoat, her hair was plastered against her cheeks.

His own shoes were soaked through at this point, squishing with every step. "Sure, we're good."

Her eyes narrowed slightly as she slowed on the trail. "That sounds more like a question."

"Fine, I'm a little turned around."

She snickered slightly, her annoyance fading. "Was it that hard to admit that you're wrong or lost?"

"Yeah, kind of."

That made her laugh even more, which in turn pulled a laugh from him. "Damn it, we're so lost. We can't be that far off track though." He sighed and looked around the woods as he adjusted his small backpack. They were on one of the trails, so really they simply had to figure out which direction to go. All the trails circled back to the same place but...this area didn't even *look* familiar. He might not be a master tracker or hiker like Mac, but still, he should recognize the area.

"Maybe we should try using GPS on our phones or something," Marcy suggested as she walked up ahead a little ways, her sneakers making squishing sounds.

"I don't know if it'll help all the way out here." It was just sprinkling now so he pulled his phone out and realized that he had no service. There was a big fat X where the bars normally were. *Damn it.*

"Hey, that kind of looks like four-wheeler tracks." She pointed into the woods.

He frowned at the makeshift trail with fresh tire tracks, only slightly filled with water. "Come on."

He brushed his wet hair out of his face and headed down the trail, wincing at all the mud. Hopefully this would take them back to civilization. Or at least somewhere that he could figure out their location and make it back home.

As they headed down the trail, their boots sucking down each step they took, he grasped her hand in his. "It could be worse, right?"

"Yeah, I could be in dry clothes right now and drinking a hot cup of coffee."

He laughed, something he did a lot with her. "True. But at least we're together."

"No one I'd rather be with. When we get back, I say we grab a hot shower before anything else." Her voice dropped slightly and just like that his entire body reacted. Which was pretty standard when he was with Marcy. He'd just turned nineteen and hadn't thought he wanted anything serious while in college, but after meeting her, he'd been hooked.

He nodded. "Deal." As they continued down the trail, he saw old pieces of plywood nailed to some of the oak trees about fifteen feet up. Flecks of red paint were peeling off them but he couldn't make out the words. If he had to guess, however, they'd likely once said something along the lines of *Keep Out*. He paused and pointed upward. "I think I know where we are. I think this is our back neighbor's property."

"Neighbor?"

"They're not technically our neighbors, but I don't know what else to call them. The people who own the property behind us. I don't know who they are though. I remember Mac talking about an asshole who used to live near here, but that was years ago." The guy had gone to prison or something.

A distant gunshot blast through the air and they both stilled. His heart rate kicked up, not from the gun-shot—he heard those enough out in the country.

"Think someone's hunting?" Marcy whispered, her hands tightening on her backpack straps.

He glanced up at the darkening sky, the gray clouds rolling in promising more rain. "Maybe." It was still general gun season and would be for a few more weeks, but... "Hunters are going to come out after the rain when the animals are moving. Not now."

There was another shot, quickly followed by a *rat-a-tat-tat*. He reached for her hand and tugged her off the trail.

"That's not a hunting rifle." He might not hunt, but he was familiar enough with what normal hunting shots sounded like. There'd be one, maybe two or three in a row if the hunter missed the first time. That sounded...like a semiautomatic. "I want to get off this trail," he said, keeping his voice low. "I don't know what that is, but I say we head south. Eventually it should take us back to my house." He really, really hoped so anyway.

She nodded, her green eyes trusting, and he hated that he'd gotten them so damn lost. He hadn't even wanted to come out and should have just said so.

At least their shoes weren't sticking in the thick tracks anymore, just squishing over the grass of the high ground. As they hurried through the woods, he tried to ignore the rumble of thunder overhead. Through the trees above he could see the dark gray clouds rolling over them. Yeah, it was about to get worse before it got better.

Then...he held out his hand at the sound of distant voices. The soft patter of rain and another rumble made it hard to tell exactly where the voices were coming from.

Marcy stilled next to him, her expression tense as she looked around.

Two men were talking nearby.

She held a finger up to her lips and motioned that she would stay quiet. He nodded and they both crept forward toward the sound of the voices. If it was just hunters, they'd ask for directions and get out of here. But he wanted to be careful since those gunshots had been abnormal for the area. The farther they walked, the more the trees thinned and the louder the voices grew.

As they reached the edge of the clearing, he grabbed her hand and tugged her down behind a bunch of overgrown brush.

Staying hidden, he peered through the thick grass and azalea bushes. The rain was picking up again but he could see two men standing on a makeshift front porch attached to a double-wide trailer. One had on a T-shirt and jeans, the other a tank top and what looked like boxer shorts. Tank top guy had a mask shoved up on top of his head as he argued with the one wearing jeans.

"What if someone heard!" the guy in the boxers shouted.

The man in the jeans held out a hand. "No one's out here! No one can hear us, dumbass. Which is exactly why we're running our business out here."

Business? Joe eyed the trailer again, noticed that all the windows were open even though it was cold and rainy out. Dark curtains fluttered in the wind. And there was a pile of respiratory masks spilling over one of the open garbage bins. Trash littered the left side of the house, the two bins completely full. Plastic soda bottles with tubes coming out of them stuck out of one of the bins and what looked like some kind of makeshift ventilation fan was on the roof.

Ohhhhhh, shit. A meth house.

Panic set in as realization hit. Meth dealers were paranoid lunatics. And these guys had semiautomatic weapons. *Oh, hell no.*

They had to get out of here. He grabbed Marcy's hand and squeezed once.

Fear in her gaze, she nodded and they both slowly crawled backward as another rumble of thunder rolled across the sky. Rain started falling harder now, drowning out their movements as they finally shoved up and started running.

Once they'd been moving for a solid ten minutes, she slowed, breathing hard. "That was a meth house, right?"

He nodded, the gears in his brain working. At least he had a good idea where they were now. Unfortunately. *Ugh.*

"Should we call the sheriff?" she asked.

"I want to talk to Mac first. I don't actually know if this is Sheriff Jordan's territory. I think it might be under the jurisdiction of a neighboring police department."

"Why can't we contact them?"

"Because I'm pretty sure the chief owns that property." Which was why he wanted to talk to his brother first. He needed advice before he did something stupid and made the wrong call.

CHAPTER FOUR

Adeline stepped out of the hallway, instinctively glancing around for Mac in the kitchen as she inhaled the rich aroma of coffee. Before pouring herself a mug, however, she moved through the house, hoping he hadn't left.

She didn't think he would have just dipped out before she'd woken up, but the rain had stopped sometime in the night or early morning, so maybe he had. She strode out to the living room and froze at the sight before her. Mac had his back to her, the drapes were open, and he was *shirtless*, thank you very much, as he looked out over the pristine, glistening lake.

She must have made a noise because he turned, his eyes going heavy-lidded for a moment, but then just as quickly he gave her a small smile. "Morning," he rumbled.

He looked sexy in the morning, sounded sexy... Oh, she was in trouble. "Morning," she rasped out, then cleared her throat. "How long have you been up?"

"Couple hours."

She blinked. "Seriously?"

He lifted a shoulder and absently rubbed a hand down his six-pack. Was he trying to kill her right now? "Yeah. Couldn't turn my brain off. I worry about my brothers."

41

"I imagine so after what happened with Joe." He'd been lost for days, knocked unconscious and left to float in a cold lake. He'd rebounded fast once he'd been rescued, but she'd been there that day, had seen him close to death's door.

Mac nodded as if he wanted to say more, but turned away again, looking back out at the lake. It was like a sheet of glass stretching out in one gorgeous pane.

But her focus wasn't on nature. Nope, it was on the man in front of her. She tried not to ogle all the ripped muscles of his back. She failed spectacularly. "I can't believe how much it cleared up overnight." Adeline moved up to the window, sliding in next to him. She tried to subtly inhale that earthy, rich scent of his without looking like an obvious weirdo.

"We should get a reprieve for about an hour or two but the report says it's supposed to rain again. I was just going to grab some coffee before heading out."

Her stomach muscles tightened. She didn't want him to leave—for multiple reasons. He made her feel safe and...she liked him a lot. "Look, you don't have to leave. And if you're insistent on going, do you want to at least do something fun first? Maybe take the canoe out?" She knew he liked water-themed activities and she'd been a little nervous about getting the big canoe down from the boathouse by herself anyway. And, okay, she wanted to hang out with him a little more. It was impossible to deny at this point. Having him under the same roof last night had solidified it.

He paused and she thought for sure he was going to say no, but he nodded. "You're sure?"

"Yes. This place is big enough for the two of us."

"I meant about taking the canoe out. I'm still going to head out today. I know it's been a rough year for you and—"

Oh no, she so didn't want to talk about her kidnapping. "You're a frustrating man, Mac Collins," she murmured as she stepped back. "I'm going to grab some coffee and change. Want to meet me back here in ten minutes?" And dear God, she hoped he put a shirt on. Or maybe she didn't.

The look he gave her was...heated. Yep, that was the word. "Sure."

As she hurried back to the bedroom, she had to remind herself that the last man she'd gotten involved with had been an abusive nightmare—and that was the understatement of the century. She still had the scars to prove it.

She liked Mac, and deep down she knew he was nothing like her ex. She wasn't that stupid, naive girl anymore, and Mac made her feel safe on a fundamental level. But in order to be in a relationship, she would have to make herself vulnerable, open up. Maybe not share all her secrets—like the very big one that had helped shape her—but she'd still have to be honest about who she was. At least if she wanted the relationship to go anywhere.

For some reason the thought of opening up to Mac didn't completely horrify her, and that alone was a scary thing. Because he was the kind of man she could fall for hard and fast. And that was the kind of fall you didn't get up from and just dust yourself off when things went south.

No, it was the kind that broke you.

And she wasn't sure she was ready for that risk. Mac might make her feel safe, but taking a risk with him was anything but that.

* * *

"You plan on helping?" Mac bit back a laugh as Adeline stood on the dock of the boathouse, hands on hips, watching him hoist the canoe down from its hooks.

"You really seem like you have it under control." In jeans, a formfitting sweater with a sparkly snowman on the front and a sparkly cap, her dark curls bouncing out from underneath, she was...perfection.

He forced his gaze away from her so he wouldn't stare. "So is this how this morning's going to go? I'm going to be the only one paddling?" He kept his voice light, playful. Because damn, she just brought out that side of him. He felt younger around her, as if the weight of running his own business, raising his brothers, just...maybe not faded away completely, but she made him feel alive in a way he hadn't felt in years.

"Well, if you're going to volunteer." She laughed lightly and grabbed two oars off the wall rack. "I'm kidding. I just figured I'd get in the way. And it looks awkward and heavy," she added, giving him a cheeky smile.

He'd noticed the way she'd been eyeing his biceps when he'd hefted the thing down, and he could admit that he liked the way she'd been watching him wayyyy too much. He felt like things had shifted between them last night—or maybe he was just projecting what he wanted. But things felt different somehow. Easier.

She joked around with him, had invited him to stay a couple hours longer—so she wasn't trying to avoid him. And he'd given her an easy out, telling her that he'd be leaving. This shift gave him hope that he might have a chance with her.

And he'd decided that she was adorable all the time. Hell, sexy and adorable, which seemed at odds, but there it was. It was all the sparkles, he thought. She was always sparkling, and didn't seem to care what anyone thought of her. Today she had on purple sequined sneakers. She had them in almost every color—and he noticed everything about her. When she'd been coming to tutor his brother he'd sort of kept track, seeing if there was a pattern to which color she wore which day. Because he found everything about her fascinating.

"What's that look?" She frowned at him as he eased the canoe into the bay. The dock and boathouse were sturdy, with a roof that looked brand-new. Derek and Madison clearly took care to clean this place out regularly, or had a property management company that did.

"Just hoping your shoes don't get ruined," he murmured as he straightened.

She shrugged. "Doesn't matter if they get wet. These are on their last leg anyway. It's why I brought them on this getaway."

"You want to climb in first? Then I can push off?"

She nodded and jumped into the front, moving like a nimble cat. The water barely rippled underneath the boat.

Laughing lightly, he followed suit and got in behind her. Sunlight hit his face as they paddled out of the boathouse, gliding onto the pristine lake.

That was one thing about Florida weather—it turned on a dime. Last night had been National Geographic scary, and today the water was like glass and there were no clouds in the sky. Though he knew they only had a couple hours before the weather shifted again.

"So how are your brothers doing without you?" she asked as she slipped her life jacket on.

He kept his on the seat next to him. "I'm sure they're fine. I lost service sometime last night. Still haven't gotten it back."

"Yeah, I alternate between one bar and zero. Guessing the storm knocked a tower out." She turned her face up to the sun and let her paddle sit still for a moment.

He watched the way her curls gleamed under the sunlight and wished he had the right to run his fingers through them, to cup her head as he took her mouth. "So do you kayak or canoe much?"

"Not really. Though Bianca's gotten me out on the water a few times. She's an avid kayaker."

He sliced his oar through the water and she did the same. "I didn't think you liked her." Mac might not pay attention to everything in town, but he did pay attention to anything involving Adeline.

She let out a surprised laugh, the musical sound echoing over the lake. "We definitely didn't always get along. Though I didn't know you were aware of that." She glanced over her shoulder, her brown eyes curious.

"I notice things."

She paused and turned back around, continuing to slice her paddle through the water.

A few birds swooped overhead and he inhaled the crisp winter air. The winter down here was a whole lot different than up north. It wasn't a biting cold, even in December, but it was crisp and refreshing. There was a reason so many people retired to the state.

"Getting kidnapped with someone will definitely change things up." Her tone was neutral as she finally responded.

Oh, hell. *Way to go, dumbass.* He couldn't believe himself. "I'm sorry, I wasn't even thinking. I wasn't trying to bring that up." Bianca and Adeline had both been kidnap victims, and had thankfully both been rescued, relatively unharmed. Adeline still had some burn scars on her arm though. Faded now, but they'd never go away.

"I know. It's fine. Talking about it actually helps. She's been someone to talk to, someone who understands what I went through because she did too. And...now that she's come out," she continued, "she's more secure in who she is. I think a lot of her mean girl attitude was a façade because she hadn't quite figured out who she was. Or she wasn't ready to tell the world anyway. Not being able to live authentically... I imagine that hurts inside and comes out in anger or other ways."

He assumed Adeline meant because Bianca had come out as gay. Before, she'd had the reputation of flirting with married men and Mac figured it was because she wasn't ready to accept who she was, and married men were safe to flirt with. Not that he was in the habit of analyzing people. Bianca had certainly never flirted with him.

"I'm glad you've got someone to talk to. If you ever need another ear, I'm here," he found himself offering. And he meant it.

"You know, from most people I would think that was a bullshit offer, but I believe you. Thanks." Turning around, she gave him a soft smile and he felt it all the way to his core as sure as if someone had sucker punched him.

Yeah, he was in trouble.

He'd known it, but today...damn. The pull he felt to her was out in the open and he couldn't rein it back in if he'd wanted to.

They paddled their way around the lake, as if they'd both made a unified decision to head left and loop all the way around.

"These homes are gorgeous," she said about ten minutes later.

The silence between them wasn't awkward, it was...*nice* out here with her. Peaceful. He'd wanted to get away from people, but Adeline definitely wasn't *people*. Being around her soothed something inside him and he wasn't sure he wanted to dig deeper into the analysis of why. Hell, he didn't have to dig deep. He knew exactly why he liked being with her.

"Yeah, Derek and Madison put a lot of work into their place too. His dad left it to him."

"That's right, I forgot you guys went to high school together."

"Yeah. He's come a long way since those days too."

"Too?"

He just snorted. Mac had been an irresponsible jackass back then—as a lot of teenagers were. Mac was glad he'd grown out of it, and that Adeline only knew him as the man he'd grown into.

He just hoped that he could be someone she relied on, turned to. Let in.

CHAPTER FIVE

Adeline looked over her shoulder as the wind suddenly shifted and that was when she saw it—behind them the sky was covered in near-black clouds, a faint strip of pale blue beneath it making it a terrifying postcard, it was so surreal. The canoe rippled against the water as more wind kicked up, shoving them hard to the west.

"Mac?" she asked as water splashed her face.

"I see it." And he was already shifting the boat back around, his forearms flexing as he sliced the oar through the water.

Following suit, she did the same, working against the wind as they maneuvered it around.

The wind kicked up again, sending a flurry of cold slicing through her as the first drop of rain hit her face. *What the hell?* It was still freaking sunny out. She cut through the water with her oar, a sense of urgency eating through her veins as they paddled. She'd thought they had plenty of time before the weather changed to get some fresh air and sunshine. Thankfully the wind was at their backs, helping to propel them forward as they quickly worked to get to their cabin.

Splat. Splat. Splat.

The rain fell harder, pelting her in the face. She winced at the stinging but kept up her pace, slice, slice,

slice. The oar slicked through the pitching water with each stroke, her arm muscles straining. With each little wave, more water sloshed into the canoe. A teeny bit of panic slid through her as she worried what would happen if they didn't make it back in time. She could swim, but it was freezing. Even if it was Florida, the water was damn cold.

Too cold for their bodies to withstand long-term.

"Here." Mac's voice made her turn. He held out his ball cap. "It'll protect your face."

"It's fine." Though the rain was cold and annoying.

Ignoring her, he put it on her head and tugged it down.

It fit perfectly so he'd clearly already changed the Velcro strap. Damn. The man was ridiculously thoughtful, and it really did help against the stinging rain. She figured his beard helped protect his face at least, and didn't feel so bad for taking his hat. She started paddling faster, squinting against the downpour as they cut straight down the middle of the lake.

A chill had started to invade her veins, but relief surged through her when she spotted the boathouse through the rain.

Dark clouds rolled over them, however. Now they were surrounded by the gray on every side. Thunder rumbled, the sound ominous, as if it was right on top of them.

They were almost there and she knew they'd be fine, but the cold from the wind and water had seeped into her bones. The tips of her fingers were numb and icy as she forced herself to keep paddling. Though deep down she knew Mac was basically carrying them at this point. The canoe was moving far too fast, an arrow through the choppy water. She felt like she was hardly helping at all.

"Put your oar down!" he called out over the rising wind.

Lightning flashed across the sky and she jumped, goose bumps skittering down her arms.

She wasn't sure why he wanted her to put the paddle down, but she pulled it in and tucked it under the seat in front of her.

He continued through the water, even faster as the canoe rocked, only twenty yards to go now. They slammed up against the boathouse dock as he guided them in.

"Sit tight," he ordered as he jumped from the boat.

She couldn't have gotten out on her own if she'd wanted to. And she *did* want to. But her fingers weren't obeying her as she fumbled to reach the side of the dock.

Suddenly Mac was next to her, slipping his big arms underneath her armpits and hauling her onto the dock. He moved with such a rapid efficiency that all she could do was stare at him as he then hooked the boat up and tossed the life jackets into the bin. Instead of securing the oars, he threw them on the dock and scooped her up into his arms.

Her teeth chattering, her jaw was tight as she tried to force words out. "What...you doing?" Well, duh. Why had she asked?

"Getting us inside." She could see chill bumps on his face and neck but he was moving so smoothly, as if he was completely impervious to the rain and wind.

She wrapped her arms around his neck, grateful for his presence and strength. She wasn't so sure she'd have made it to the house without him and that was terrifying. She was so damn cold, all her muscles pulled taut, almost locked in on themselves as she fought the iciness that invaded her marrow.

He shoved the back door open and immediately the warmth of the living room rolled over her. But he kept going, moving all the way to the bathroom where he set her on her feet and turned on the hot shower.

"You need to strip." There was a flicker of worry in his eyes.

"I'm fine," she rasped out as she fumbled with the edge of the zipper of her pants. Stupid thing wouldn't work. Yeah, clearly she was freaking *fine*. But her fingers weren't listening to her.

He took over in an instant, quickly unzipping it before he tugged her sweater over her head.

She didn't have any time to be embarrassed as he then bent down and tugged her soggy shoes and socks off—then helped pull her pants off. The man undressed her with an impressive efficiency, and thankfully didn't touch her underwear. The fact that he didn't, mattered. And he averted his gaze as she managed to unhook her bra and slide it down her arms. Chills covered her entire body, though the warmth from the house was helping already.

He looked to the right and up, not focusing on her. "Can you get in the shower without help?"

"Yeah," she got out through chattering teeth. The curtain jingled as she managed to shove it open and step inside.

The moment the warmth of the water hit her, the frostiness eating up her insides started to ease.

"Sorry," she called out, unable to form words without her teeth chattering. "I don't know how I got so chilled." Especially when he seemed to be fine. She swore it felt like it was in her marrow, the way it had invaded her so quickly.

"Don't apologize. Are you doing okay? Do you need help?"

"No, I'm good, I promise." Her words were coming out stronger now. It had just been a shock to her body.

"I'm going to take your clothes to the laundry room and clean up all the water on the floor. I'll be back in a minute. Unless you want me to stay?"

"No, I'm good, and you don't have to take my clothes." She was embarrassed that he was so strong and capable and—

"Don't be ridiculous. I've got this. I'll also start a fresh pot of coffee. You'll feel even better once you drink some."

Okay, so this man was seriously like a knight in shining armor. The mere thought of someone taking care of her, helping her like this, would have sent her running in the past. Now? She wanted to run all right, straight into his arms. "Thank you."

* * *

Adeline stepped into the kitchen minutes later, wearing a thick sweater, jogging pants and two layers of socks, to find Mac pouring two mugs of coffee. "You are a prince," she murmured as he placed the hot drink in her hands. She savored the warmth against her palms as she lifted the mug to her lips.

His eyes crinkled slightly as he smiled but his expression quickly morphed to one of concern. "How are you feeling?"

"Like a new person. And a tiny bit embarrassed that you *literally* had to carry me inside and..." She cleared her throat, deciding not to finish that he'd seen her naked. Or mostly, anyway.

His frown deepened and it just made him sexier. Apparently everything he did was sexy. "You have nothing to be embarrassed about. We shouldn't have gone out. It's my fault."

"Yeah, because you control the weather," she murmured. "If you remember correctly, it was my idea. And it's no one's fault, just dumb luck. Also, for the record, I hate Florida weather sometimes."

He picked up his own mug and leaned against the counter as he nodded in agreement. "No kidding. So I got cell service back and we've got a bunch of flash flood warnings in the area. Looks like we're stuck together for a little while longer." His tone was so neutral, she wished she could read him better.

"I can definitely think of worse things. At least we have power." Thunder rattled the house just then, making the windows shake. She winced. "You know, unless I just jinxed us."

He snorted softly. "If you want to paint or relax, I'll get out of your way."

She shrugged, not wanting to be alone right now. "Want to play some board games?"

He lifted an eyebrow. "Seriously?"

"I love them, but I get it if you don't want to. I am the queen of board games, so if you can't handle losing to a girl, I completely understand. Because I will utterly destroy you."

He blinked in surprise, then grinned. "Bring it on, then. I should warn you, I'm the undefeated champ of Monopoly with my brothers. I have a dance."

She sputtered out a laugh, not expecting this at all. "A *dance?*"

His lips twitched slightly. "That's right, my friend. A *dance*. If you're lucky, you'll get to see it."

"I'm tempted to throw the game just so I can see what this is all about."

He grinned and she felt that look aaaallllll the way to her belly. Good God, this man was her kryptonite. He was sexy, fun, had pretty much saved her from hypothermia. And earlier he'd made it clear that he still wanted to take her out on a date. There were no mind games with him. It was terrifying.

Adeline knew she needed to get over her past, needed to move forward. It was just taking that next step that was the difficult thing.

And something told her that if she took it with Mac, she wouldn't regret it. No, she would only regret it if she took a chance and then lost him.

CHAPTER SIX

Lincoln opened the front door, surprised to see Serenity, his sister-in-law, on the other side. "Hey," he said as he stepped back, letting her in.

"Hey." She hugged him quickly, a smile on her face, but he'd known her long enough to recognize the tension rolling off her. "Where's Autumn?" she asked.

"Had a little morning sickness and ended up getting back in bed."

She winced slightly. "I don't miss those days."

"Did you come by to see her, or me?" He motioned for her to follow him to the kitchen.

"Both. I mean, I came by to see you, but I was hoping to see her as well. Always," she said with a laugh. "I'm so glad you guys are together now. You're both so good for each other."

Her words made him smile. He'd been close friends with Serenity since before college so he was glad that she and Autumn were so tight. "Yeah, well I'm glad my brother finally made his move on you." Lucas had been hopeless where Serenity had been concerned. The two of them deserved all the happiness in the world. Especially after the hell she'd been through.

"Me too."

"So what's up?" Because there was no way she'd just stopped by unannounced without a reason.

"Nothing really. I'm just feeling kind of tense right now." Her blue eyes flashed with what looked like worry.

"Aren't you on vacation? Or a sort of vacation?"

She snorted softly and sat at the kitchen table, accepting the coffee he slid over to her. "Supposed to be."

"So what's going on?"

"I got a call from a friend of mine, Hope Dunaway."

"Who is she?" The name sounded vaguely familiar.

"She runs the feed store over in Harrison. I know the sheriff's department's jurisdiction is spread over multiple counties... But I also know the police department of Harrison has jurisdiction over, well, Harrison. So..." She took a sip of her coffee, her expression pensive as she watched him.

"So? Is this about the chief over there?" He tried to keep his tone as neutral as possible. But he did not like Robert "Bobby" Hayward. Never had. Lately he'd been hearing slight rumblings of...corruption. There was no other way to put it. And Hayward's son Harlan had recently gotten out of prison, but that was a whole other mess. Lincoln had also been hearing things about that jackass, but with no proof to back it up, unfortunately. Still, it was on his radar.

"Yeah. Hope's been getting hassled by some guys at work. And she's gone to the police department a couple times to try to make a report but he keeps blowing her off. Telling her that if she makes the report, it will become official. He's talking to her like she's stupid, like her 'pretty little self doesn't want to go and make trouble.'" Serenity's tone was mocking.

"The point of making reports is so they become official," he growled. The thought of any woman being disrespected—or terrorized—got his blood boiling. It wasn't going to happen on his watch.

"Exactly. She said she feels like she's banging her head against the wall. And I guess the chief is hunting buddies with the two guys, so obviously he's trying to protect them instead of doing his job. It all feels so gross and shady and she has nowhere to turn."

"She can call me anytime. Feel free to give her my cell. Or better yet... Do you think it would cause trouble for her if I stopped by the feed store?" In uniform, in his official vehicle. But only if she was okay with it. He didn't want to create more trouble for her inadvertently. But his presence could go a long way toward making this shit stop. Unfortunately, it didn't stop the long-term problem of a chief who was corrupt. But one step at a time.

"I'll call her and ask, but I know she wants to talk to you."

"You hear anything else about him?"

"No, but I'll definitely keep my ear to the ground after this. It's amazing to me, *horrifyingly* amazing, how different you guys are. I hate that she can't even trust law enforcement where she is."

"I do too." He was going to look further into this for sure. He'd already been unofficially investigating Chief Hayward a little bit—something he wasn't going to tell Serenity—but now he was going to open an official investigation into the police chief.

No one was above the law.

However, Lincoln would have to be very careful who he trusted with this information.

Autumn strode into the kitchen then, her dark hair slightly mussed and her sweater stretching across her small baby bump, making him smile.

Her face lit up as she saw Serenity. "I thought I heard you. Why didn't you wake me?" she asked Lincoln before brushing her mouth over his. Then she moved in to hug her friend.

"You needed your sleep," he said.

"He worries too much," Autumn murmured as she sat at the island next to Serenity. "Would you mind making me some tea? Decaf." She practically spit the word out as if it was poison.

Serenity wrapped an arm around her shoulders and pulled her close. "It'll get better soon, I promise."

"That's what I keep telling myself. I'm just tired all the time. I feel like an alien has taken over my body or something."

Serenity snickered. "It's because an alien *has* taken over your body. You're actually growing another person. You're going to be soooo tired for a little while, so take advantage and sleep all you can."

"I feel part-bear at this point."

Lincoln laughed lightly before starting the tea, just watching the woman he loved more than anything. Autumn had been through her own version of hell too and had come through the other side even stronger. He was so damn thankful she'd moved in next door to him—and changed his life forever.

He half listened as the women talked, and once Autumn's tea was ready he set it in front of her before kissing her on top of her head. He actually did have to get in to work and he really wanted to start digging deep into Hayward as soon as possible.

"Hey, before I forget." Serenity stopped him before he could leave the kitchen. "Adeline is off this week too. She's staying up at a lake in Clay County. We've been texting but last night I couldn't get anything to go through. And when I called it went straight to voicemail. I'm probably being paranoid. I know the rain is a bit worse up there. I'm just worried about her. Especially with her being all alone."

"Do you know where's she staying?"

"Yeah, Derek and Madison's place."

He frowned slightly as the memory of something tickled his brain. "I thought Derek said he let Mac Collins use it this week."

Serenity shook her head. "I don't know if you have your dates right, but I know she's up there. I talked to her and she was alone. Is there any way you can find out what kind of flooding they've had? Kind of maybe...get someone to check on her? But not in an obvious way like I'm checking on her? I know she can take care of herself."

"No problem. I know who runs that area. I'll reach out, see if they can do a sweep of the entire lake. We'll make sure she's okay. But with all the storms, it's very likely a couple cell towers got knocked out. That's probably the reason you can't get through."

"That's what I keep telling myself."

Lincoln headed out, already on the phone. He'd kept his tone light for Serenity, but he'd already heard from a friend who was a fireman out of Clay County that they were dealing with record flooding.

If Adeline was staying indoors, she'd be fine. He just really, really hoped she wasn't trying to drive anywhere.

CHAPTER SEVEN

Mac watched Adeline across the table. Which wasn't hard. She was easy to look at—hell, addicting. Her hair had dried now, and all her curls were bouncy and wild—and he was obsessed with the thought of running his fingers through them as he took her mouth with his.

Sitting at the kitchen window, Adeline glanced out when a flash of lightning streaked across the sky. "So how did you get into woodwork?" Her voice was melodic and wrapped around him as she spoke.

"Are you just feigning interest so I'll ignore how badly you're destroying me?"

She grinned and fanned out her cards in front of her. "Royal flush."

He winced and tossed his own down, two pairs. "You didn't actually answer."

"No, I'm definitely interested. I've seen some of your pieces. I've even..." Clearing her throat, she grabbed the cards quickly and started shuffling them.

They'd played Monopoly, Battleship, and after she'd killed him in both—taking great joy in sinking his ships— he'd suggested poker. Apparently she was a shark at this too. And it was impressive. "You even what?"

"Nothing. You know, it's a good thing we're not playing for money, or you'd be broke." The smile she gave him was mischievous, and damn, he wanted to make her smile all the time. It was a relief that she was back to her normal self. Seeing her teeth chattering like that earlier, actually having to help her undress because she'd been so damn chilled… He'd lost a couple years of his life.

He snagged the cards from her. "It's my turn to shuffle and I'm not letting this go. What were you going to say?"

She let out a small sigh. "I was just going to say that I even went to your website because I was curious about prices, and realized that your stuff is definitely out of my budget. And the reason I stopped talking about it is because I didn't want you to think that I was like—"

"I'll make you something." He would love to make something specifically for her. And…he might have already started on something small. He'd tried to tell himself that it was just a personal project, but in the back of his mind he'd always had an intended recipient for it.

Adeline.

Her cheeks flushed as she shook her head, her dark curls bouncing. "No way. That's exactly why I stopped talking. I'm not going to take advantage of you. I can only imagine how long your wait list is."

He would love it if she took advantage of him, in a completely other way. "We'll see."

She narrowed her gaze at him before she shifted in her seat, stretching slightly.

"Are you about done with board games?"

"While beating you *is* a lot of fun," she said with a cheeky grin, "I'm getting kind of hungry for lunch and would like to get some painting in."

"Of course. I actually need to check in with my brothers and I'm going to see if I can figure out where the worst of the flooding is around here."

"I was going to make paninis in the sandwich press. I'll make one for you too if you want," Adeline said as she started cleaning up all of their games.

"That'd be great, thanks." He helped gather some of the smaller pieces and stack the boxes neatly on a nearby bookshelf.

Once he was done, Mac headed out onto the back patio, standing under the overhang so he wouldn't get wet. Dark gray clouds blanketed the sky. Though the rain was now at a drizzle, flashes of sporadic heat lightning lit up the sky.

Sighing, he looked back down at his phone, hoping for service just as it started buzzing with incoming text messages.

Call me, I have a question. The first was from Joe.

You okay? We can't get through. Now Dylan.

Not trying to bug you, just wanted to ask you something. Joe again.

Then there were three more from Joe, which definitely wasn't like him. The messages were all benign enough but his brothers rarely checked in anymore. They were older and spreading their wings and this…felt off.

Mac called Joe back first since he'd sent the most messages.

"Hey," his brother answered on the first ring.

"What's up?"

He just jumped right into it. "Marcy and I were out for a hike this morning on the property."

Instinctively, Mac winced. Joe went out hiking with him in the fall but he was definitely more of an indoor type of guy. Gaming and design were his loves and he was good at them. Outdoor stuff, not so much.

"Pretty sure we ran across a meth house on the neighboring property," Joe continued, his words rushed and tight.

Mac stilled, afraid to move and lose service now. "How do you even know what a meth house looks like?"

"I learned about it in one of my elective classes. A criminal justice one—and come on, man, I watch TV."

Jesus. A meth house. Mac rubbed a hand over his face.

"I think it's on that property that neighbors us, the one owned by the Haywards."

He bit back a curse. "Yeah, I don't know if it's changed hands or anything in recent years." He'd heard that Harlan Hayward had gotten out of jail a few months ago, but hadn't thought too much about it. The guy was a piece of crap, a blast from Mac's past that he never wanted to think about again. At one time they'd more or less run with the same crowd but that had been so long ago Mac didn't even recognize the boy he'd been back then.

"I didn't know if I should tell Sheriff Jordan about what I saw or...what. I don't actually have the coordinates or anything and I was trespassing. Not on purpose, but still. And I didn't even think to take pictures or anything. It was raining and we'd gotten lost. I just wanted to get us out of there. I was...I was scared for both of us."

"You did the right thing. Seriously, meth dealers are beyond dangerous. Sit tight and I'll call Lincoln directly, let him know what you saw. But I want to go with you when you talk to him." Mac wasn't letting Joe deal with this by himself.

"I can talk to him on my own." There was just a hint of petulance in his tone.

"I *know*. But I don't want you making an official statement right now. I'm not sure what the protocol is and I don't want to call 911. I don't want this on a recorded line. This isn't about your capability or anything. I want to speak to Lincoln in person, and off the record. So just sit tight." Because meth dealers could be violent and vengeful. He wasn't letting Joe get tangled up in that.

"Okay. When are you coming home?"

"I'm not sure yet." He'd planned to head home tomorrow—he'd only wanted a couple days away. But with the flooding he was thinking he and Adeline might need to leave now and find a way out of here so they could actually get home instead of being trapped here for even longer. Even if he loved being under the same roof with her. The longer they stayed, the worse it could get. "But cell service is spotty so if you don't hear from me, don't worry." He paused. "I'm with Adeline."

"For real? How's she doing?"

"Good. Turns out this place got more or less double-booked by Derek and his wife. They screwed up the dates and we both ended up here at the same time."

"I miss seeing her all the time but I'm glad that class is over. Tell her I said hey."

"I will." Once they disconnected, he called Sheriff Jordan immediately. It went straight to voicemail so he hung up instead of leaving a message. Then he simply texted him, letting Lincoln know he needed to talk. That would have to do for now because he wasn't putting anything in writing regarding Harlan Hayward and a meth house. Hell no.

Next he called the local PD to get information on where all the flooding was. He was getting Adeline out of here ASAP.

Because no way was he leaving her behind.

CHAPTER EIGHT

Harlan slowed his four-wheeler, looking at different tracks in the thick mud. Glancing over his shoulder, he saw that Billy Ray did the same, skidding slightly at an angle into the underbrush.

"What is it?" Billy Ray called out, pushing the bill of his ball cap up slightly. The rain had started up again, just drizzling now, but they were going to be in for another couple hours of hard rain soon.

Instead of answering, Harlan slid off his four-wheeler and stomped through the mud, frowning at the clear footprints leading down the trail. They disappeared into the woods, but he could see where water was filling them up. "You been out here on foot lately?" he asked as Billy Ray came up to stand next to him. The man smelled like onions and tobacco, but Harlan kept that thought to himself for now and took a step to the side as he tried to breathe through his mouth.

"No." Billy, a distant cousin of his, crouched down, and even though he could be a dumbass, Billy Ray had to spot the tracks too. They were *right* there.

Damn it!

People who picked up product from them never came this way, they drove in from the main road. Which was from a different direction. These tracks were out on their trail where they ran security to make sure the cops or competitors didn't try to ambush them.

"You think it's the cops?" Billy Ray asked.

"Maybe." Though his instinct was to say no. Harlan's father was the chief of police and didn't mess with any of this area. He'd given the property to Harlan recently, just signed it over and told him that he'd lost a lot of years, that he wanted Harlan to have a fresh start. While Harlan didn't think his father knew what he was doing out here, it was only because he didn't want to know. His father loved to bury his head in the sand about shit—which was good for him.

"What about neighbors?"

"We don't have any neighbors." Though he knew the asshole who owned the property behind his own. But there was a solid fifty acres separating them. Nah, that asshole Mac Collins wouldn't be back here messing around with him. Apparently he was some big shot who made fancy wood art pieces now or something. Whatever. People just loved to spend money on stupid shit— thankfully his customers did.

But someone had been back here. Recently.

"There are two sets of footprints. One smaller than the other." It was just too damn hard to really make them out. They were shaped like sneakers, but...too much water had washed away any type of shoe print or anything useful.

"What're you gonna do?"

"Follow them for now." And see where they led.

Twenty minutes later, he'd lost the trail as the rain picked up again. And it didn't tell him anything at all.

There was a chance it was the Feds. His operation was growing and he knew that the DEA and cops didn't want them moving meth through this area. But it was a moneymaker and he'd been in prison for so long. He had a lot of time to make up for, and a lot of money to earn. He sure as hell wasn't going back to prison and he wasn't going to work some bullshit office job—not that he could get one anyway. And no way in hell was he going to get into construction and break his back for little more than minimum wage.

He slid onto his four-wheeler and glanced at Billy Ray. "Head back to the trailer."

It was time to do some shopping. He had a few cameras set up, but he needed to set up more, as well as a couple traps. More than he already had. He was going to find out who the hell was sniffing around his property in one way or another.

And make sure they didn't make that mistake more than once.

He'd killed before. He'd do it again, no problem. People didn't cross him and get away with it.

CHAPTER NINE

Mac stepped through the back door to be greeted with a delicious aroma that smelled a lot like a local Italian restaurant he frequented.

"I hope you're hungry," Adeline said as he made his way into the kitchen. She'd pulled her curls back into a ponytail, and they bounced out everywhere behind her head.

"I am." For more than food. "What is all this?" She'd said she was making paninis but he'd expected something simpler. This…was mouthwatering.

"Red onions, baby bella mushrooms, sun-dried tomatoes, spinach, goat cheese and a little bit of olive oil and balsamic vinegar. I've also got a special sauce that I make myself that gives it even more flavor. I sauteed the veggies before adding them to the ciabatta bread. It all melts together in perfect panini goodness."

His stomach rumbled in response. "Well it smells amazing." And he really, really didn't want to leave. But he knew they needed to. If the flooding got worse, they could be stuck here too long and run out of supplies.

She must have read his expression because she paused as she turned off the sandwich press. "What is it? Everything okay?"

"Yeah, but I just got off the phone with the local PD. There's only one way out of here right now. The two other access roads are completely flooded. Technically there's a fourth road we could use, but we'd have to go three hours north, loop back down to the highway, and it would take another three on top of that just to get to Verona Bay. And there's no guarantee that access road will stay open anyway." And he wasn't going to gamble with something like that.

"That doesn't sound good." She slid his plate over to him, frowning slightly.

"They said if we want to leave and make it back to Verona Bay by Christmas, we should get out of here by this afternoon. It's supposed to rain another foot alone this evening."

"Yeah, I saw the weather alert, but I was hoping the roads would still be all right. I think I'll just stay the rest of the week, then. I planned on it anyway."

"Then I'll stay too." No way in hell was he leaving her here alone in these uncertain conditions.

She frowned at him as she picked up her panini. "You don't have to."

"I don't like the thought of you being stuck out here with no way to get home. I know you're capable, but what happens if you get hurt? Or run out of food? The roads to the nearest grocery store are included in that flooded list. You really want to get stuck eating gas station food if you can get it? Anything could happen out here. It's remote. And what if you lose power? There's a generator in the garage but you don't have any gas for it."

As if to punctuate his words, thunder rumbled in the distance.

"What else did law enforcement say?" she asked.

"That's about it, really. They said most locals have stocked up with food and have prepped like they do for hurricane season. The issue they're having is the lack of drainage around here. And because it's not a bigger area that brings in a lot of taxes, it's low on everyone's priority. They didn't say those words but I know what they meant. The drainage sucks here and there's simply nowhere for that much water to go. The ground is saturated and can't absorb it anymore."

She bit her bottom lip, looking adorable as she glanced around the kitchen. "I actually don't like the thought of being stuck out here alone either. I don't have a ton of dry goods because I'd planned to go to the local grocery store. But...I don't even know if my car will make it."

"We'll head out together and come back and get your car in a couple weeks. My Bronco should be able to handle the road they described. It's not standing water— yet. If we're going to leave, it needs to be today."

She sighed and nudged his plate again. "At least eat first. Then we can clean up and get out of here. What do you think, an hour?"

"That should be good."

"If we have enough time, I'll wash the sheets and at least throw them in the dryer. I think Derek and Madison will understand if we don't stay and put everything up perfectly."

"They definitely will. I actually got a text from Derek and he said to get out of here. He said not to worry about cleaning up."

"Okay." Picking up her panini, she took a bite, but he could tell she was disappointed.

Mac hated that she had to cut her vacation short, but he wanted her safe.

As he ate, he glanced down at his phone, hoping for a text from Lincoln, who he also needed to talk to. But his phone was back to having no bars. That was another reason he needed to get home. Something like a meth house relatively close to his home was bad in so many ways. It attracted paranoid, violent people.

Yep, they definitely needed to get out of here.

* * *

"It looks like a hurricane came through here." Originally from Miami, Adeline had lived through more hurricanes than she wanted to think about. But being out here in the country it seemed almost worse as she looked at all the fallen trees and branches littering the roads. It was like a bomb had exploded, sending branches flying everywhere.

"While you were packing up, I heard that at least one tornado touched down about twenty miles north of us." Mac's hands were firmly on the steering wheel as he guided them down the rain-slicked two-lane road.

"Well, I'm glad to be leaving with you," she murmured, more to herself than him. But she was. She didn't love that they'd left in such a rush—she hated not being able to leave the house exactly as they'd found it. But after she'd packed her bags and painting supplies, Mac had quickly loaded up everything into the back of his Bronco.

It was weird to leave her car behind, but she didn't mind renting a car or just walking everywhere back home. The thought of risking staying there, getting stuck in the rain even longer... That would make for a pretty crappy Christmas. Not to mention she would have run out of groceries soon enough anyway. Returning home was the right choice and she felt safe with him.

"I'm glad you came with me too." He slowed as they reached a slight bend in the road. Water rolled over the upcoming bridge, if it could even be considered a bridge. It spanned maybe two vehicle lengths.

Mac slowed more, his knuckles whitening.

"What are you thinking?" She glanced through the back window. No one was behind them because no one else was on the road.

"It's not deep, and the tires can take it." He glanced at her and gave her a look that warmed her from the inside out. She wasn't sure what it was, but his eyes sort of softened in this sweet way as if he was trying to comfort her. "I just want to keep you safe," he said before turning his attention back to the road.

Everything inside her flared to life at his words. The raw sincerity behind them.

Mac really was a good person. He hadn't made her feel weird or awkward during their time at the cabin. He wasn't nearly as stoic or even surly as he might put on for the rest of the world. He was simply reserved, kept walls up, something she understood more than most. Though she'd let down a whole lot of them since settling in Verona Bay. The people she'd bonded with had made it easy to want to settle here, to make a life. To put down roots so deep she would never want to leave. And Mac tempted her in a way no one had. She wanted to let him in, to see if the attraction between them could be more. She was just scared, plain and simple. Not of him, but of what would happen if she took the chance and lost.

"Thank you," she murmured, that warmth settling inside her even as the rain picked up, drumming against the hood and windshield.

Mac pressed the gas, gaining speed slightly as he eased them over the bridge.

As soon as they made it over the small bridge, with only a slight shaking of the Bronco, Adeline let out a breath she hadn't realized she'd been holding.

Rain pounded against the windshield in a staccato beat. It wasn't terrible enough that they couldn't see, but a deep gray, almost black, coated the sky, thick layers of rolling clouds spreading out in all directions.

The real rain was coming again. Soon. And she wanted to be a lot closer to home when that happened.

Everything seemed worse now that they were out on the open roads. Or two-lane highway, to be more accurate. It felt desolate despite all the lush greenery surrounding them on either side. Houses separated by at least an acre dotted this stretch, and most of the yards had growing pools of water in them. "It must be lower-lying land here," she murmured. It hadn't looked that bad when she'd driven in days ago.

"We just got a whole lot of rain the last couple days. There's nowhere for it to go and it's coming down too fast to soak in." His voice was tense as he eyed the road and sky in front of them.

The silence between them was comfortable as he continued driving. Neither one of them had turned on the radio and she certainly wasn't going to, wanting him to be able to concentrate on the slick roads in front of them. "It's weird being the only people on the road right now," she said.

"Yeah. Everyone else is smarter and staying inside," he said dryly.

She snorted softly. "Did you tell your brothers you're on your way home?"

"I tried to call them, couldn't get any service."

She looked at her own phone. "Same deal here."

A sudden gust of wind whipped up, slamming into the Bronco, making it tremble as the bottom of the sky finally fell out.

Her heart jumped in her throat as a deluge of water slammed against the windshield, so thick and heavy the windshield wipers were barely any help.

Mac cursed slightly but his grip was steady and he simply slowed his pace, inching down the road.

Her first instinct was to ask if they should pull over, but on this road, there was simply nowhere to go. On either side were two ditches filled with water—spilling over onto the road.

"The final bridge out of here is a mile away. We'll make it," he said into the quiet cabin of the vehicle.

His words were calm and soothing and she guessed that he'd been a really good father figure to his brothers. He seemed good in a crisis. "You don't have to try and keep me calm," she said. "Though I do appreciate it."

"Maybe I'm trying to keep myself calm."

Somehow she doubted that. The man had been in the Marines—she'd seen pictures of him in uniform when she'd been tutoring his brother. And he never seemed rattled by anything. He was like this giant, steady oak tree who weathered things and grew stronger from them. "Well, you seem like you're totally in control."

He grinned, those full lips curving up ever so slightly, though he never took his eyes off the road in front of them. Not that either of them could see much of it.

The windshield wipers made a fast *swish-swish* sound as the rain slammed against the roof, the pings overly loud, making her feel as if they were in a tin box.

She wiped her damp palms on her jeans. She wanted to be home, wanted Mac to be home, simply wanted them to be safe and warm and dry. Anywhere but here.

"So are you ready for Christmas?" she asked to keep things light. "Bought all your presents?" The questions seemed inane but she had the urge to talk now. To do anything but obsess about the storm raging outside.

"Already got both my brothers' gifts. But knowing them, they'll both wait until the last minute, likely December twenty-fourth, to buy their gifts. Though I know

Joe has been looking at some jewelry for Marcy. I just hope it's not a ring. Don't get me wrong, I like Marcy but they're so young."

"Nineteen *is* very young to be thinking about rings," she said on a laugh even as she tried not to jump as another gust of wind rattled his Bronco.

"Yeah, but at that age you think you know everything. Or at least I did."

She snorted, some of the tension in her chest easing, but not by much. "I certainly did. Nothing my mom said could convince me otherwise either."

"What about your dad?"

"He was an artist too, or at least that's what he liked to call himself. I met him all of once in my entire life. He was useless, as my mama used to say." A feckless man who hadn't taken any responsibility for becoming a parent. "He sculpted occasionally, but mainly he let rich widows take care of him—until they got tired of him and kicked him out. Last I heard he's in Boca Raton. My life is definitely better without him in it, I have no doubt. That man would have just caused heartache for me." And she'd had enough of that, thank you very much.

"That's very…evolved."

"There are some things you can change in life and some things you can't. And there are some people who will simply never be what you want them to be. I learned that lesson very young." And she was grateful for it. "I didn't always agree with the things my mom said or did, but cutting him out of our lives—not that we had to try hard—was the best thing she ever did for both of us. I just wish I'd been smart enough to listen when she told me to cut my ex out of my life." God, did she ever. Things would be so, so different now if she had. Her mother would still be alive.

Adeline swallowed one of her worst memories, buried it for now.

"Feel like expanding?" Mac's deep voice was soothing as he maneuvered through a big puddle with ease, driving in the middle of the road where the water was the lowest.

Rain continued to slam against the Bronco, and even though Adeline didn't want to open up any more, she decided to push forward. She'd brought it up for a reason. Maybe she *did* want to open up to him. "My first boyfriend, my first real one, was a nightmare. And I'm not saying that facetiously. My mom knew that, but nothing she said could convince me otherwise. I thought she was jealous, that she wanted what I had. 'True love,'" she said in a mocking tone, hating who she'd been back then.

She tried so hard to be forgiving of herself, to remind herself how young she'd been, but it didn't always help. Her stupid choices had gotten her mom killed.

"In reality, what I had was a lot of crap. And my mom was old enough to see through a thirty-year-old man who was pursuing an eighteen-year-old as hard as he did." A tight ball of tension coiled inside her as she thought of her ex. What he'd done—what *she'd* done. Her throat tightened as a wave of memories swelled up, threatening to choke her.

"I'm sorry. I made some pretty stupid decisions when I was young too. I think part of it's just the pains of growing up."

"I just wish the growing-up part was a little bit easier." And with fewer scars. "He…" She swallowed hard, wondering if she should tell him what had happened. Not all of it, but part of it. Some deeply hidden part of her wanted Mac to know this. Wanted him to know this part of her.

"It's okay if you don't want to talk about it. I don't want to cause you any pain."

Well that settled it. "No, I'd like to talk about it, if you want to hear it. It's a lot, fair warning."

"I want to hear anything and everything you have to say."

Oh God. This man. She cleared her throat, tried to emotionally steel herself as she forced the words out. "My ex was abusive. You've seen the scars on my back?" She knew he had, but wanted to confirm.

He nodded, his jaw tight.

"I finally got smart enough to break up with him. This was before the scars, but…" She cleared her throat again. "It was such a relief to be free. I didn't realize how much of my life I'd changed because of him. Seriously, it was like getting out of a prison, is the only way I can think to describe it. Just one without actual bars or shackles. He did not take my breakup well. Said I should be grateful he was even with me, that I was going nowhere—typical crap from a man who sold drugs."

Mac shot her a sideways glance, surprise flickering in his eyes.

"Yeah, he was a drug dealer too. The whole package," she said sarcastically. "I didn't know that when we first got together though. I didn't even realize it until my mom pointed out that he had a lot of money coming in and no real job. I'd just assumed he was a trust fund kid, honestly. But nope." She sighed, the words coming out easier now. "Anyway, he surprised me at my mom's house one night, busted in and tried to drag me out by my hair. It was…terrifying and awful and I still occasionally have nightmares about it."

"Jesus," Mac murmured. "I'm so sorry."

"It gets worse. You sure you want to hear it all?"

"Adeline." There was a wealth of emotion in that one word. He did want to hear what she had to say, because he cared.

Yep, this man had the power to hurt her in a way her ex never had. "My mom went at him like a banshee. She attacked him and then so did I. But he had a gun, and a gun wins against two unarmed women. He…killed my mom." Tears stung her eyes so she looked out the window. Or tried to. The rain created a blurred tapestry even after she'd wiped her tears away.

Mac sucked in a breath, but she pushed on, wanting to get all of this out.

"I managed to take him off guard, to shove him off me and run. He slipped in her…blood. He fell and I ran for all I was worth. And I didn't look back. A neighbor had already called the cops and by the time they got there, he was gone."

"Did they catch him?"

"No."

He swore again.

"They think he's dead though." She knew for a fact that he was. "There's still a warrant out for his arrest, but he's never resurfaced again. He had a lot of enemies. Around the time of...what happened, he was at war with another drug dealer. After he disappeared, that man took over his territory. The cops seem pretty sure that he was killed in their war and his body disposed of in a way that will never be found."

"I'm sorry about your mom. Sorry you lived through that hell."

"Thank you."

There was nothing else to say after that and she was glad he'd just listened. Truly, utterly listened.

As they took another bend, she knew where they were, remembered coming this way. They'd be to the main highway soon and then it should be smooth sailing—relatively speaking. They just needed to get to the highway and off these low-lying roads.

The falling rain was a heavy blanket in front of them and she gripped the handle on the door, her fingers digging into the leather and plastic.

"This is the final bridge," he murmured.

She gripped even tighter as he eased onto the bridge.

The Bronco slid slightly, the tires losing traction.

Adeline forgot to breathe, her chest tight as Mac white-knuckled the steering wheel.

Hunched forward, he steered the vehicle the last few feet across and she finally collapsed back against the seat. "I don't understand why they don't build those bridges higher."

"It's like that all over the state. Some of the older ones are still at sea level."

"If this was a different area, I guarantee the state would put more money into fixing the roads and bridges."

"No shit," he muttered. "It's ridiculous."

On the side of the road, dirt flew up everywhere and a tree split down the middle as a bright, blinding burst exploded. The noise was almost deafening, shaking her to her bones.

Her mouth fell open as the tree began to fall. She spun in her seat to stare as Mac kept going. "That...was lightning?" Her entire body was shaking. Of course it was, but she was having a hard time processing what she'd just seen and heard. Being that close to something that powerful... She swallowed hard.

"Yeah." The word came out tight as he pressed on the gas slightly. "We've got maybe half an hour until we're back in Verona Bay. We're going to make it."

She wondered if his words were for her or himself. She swallowed hard and turned around to see if she could spot the fallen tree but the rain had picked up again and it was too thick to see far.

As they rounded another bend, a sudden rush of water flowed over a small bridge. There was nowhere for them to go, no time to stop. Her heart leapt into her throat.

"Shit!" The curse tore from Mac.

Adeline braced herself as Mac pressed the brakes. But it was too late.

The Bronco fishtailed even as Mac struggled with the wheel.

She had her feet shoved up against the footwell and was grabbing onto the "oh shit" handle as the water whipped them sideways.

The curses kept flowing as they tumbled over the side, hood first.

"Mac!"

"It's okay." His voice was tight as they slammed forward into a ditch. The Bronco shuddered under the running water around it, but she realized that it wasn't filling up. They were just stuck.

Her heart rate evened out a little even as he unstrapped. "Come on, we're gonna have to climb out the back. I'll try calling a tow truck, but...we might have to hoof it."

He went out first so she grabbed her purse and slung it across her body before following. As she crawled upward on the seat because of the angle, she realized why he'd gone first. He was standing in knee-deep water, his hands up and ready.

Rain hit her in the face as she struggled to climb out.

"You got it." There he was again with the steady voice, standing there impervious to the rain and rushing water.

She tried to climb somewhat gracefully but ended up tripping on herself and falling into his waiting arms. Because of course she did.

A new deluge of water fell and he wrapped his arms around her. "Come on. We've just got to make it over there." He pointed but she could barely see.

Good thing he knew what he was doing. Water weighed her legs down, but she shoved onward until her feet hit squishy, mushy...grass?

"Come on." He still had a grip on her and that was when she saw the two-story house. "We'll see if they can help us."

As they reached the front steps, the door swung open and a woman with dark brown skin and salt-and-pepper hair, who Adeline guessed to be in her seventies, opened it before they could even think about knocking. "Oh, look at you two. Come on in, get out of the rain."

Adeline wasn't sure if it was everything that had happened or if maybe she was raw from telling Mac one of her most guarded secrets, but she burst into tears.

The woman made a clucking sound even as Mac made a distressed one, but she didn't care. She wanted to be dry, home, and in her own bed. Maybe with Mac right next to her.

* * *

Forty minutes later, Adeline was dry and a little more centered as she sat at the round kitchen table of Flora Whitten, a retiree who'd been living in this house for forty years. She'd let them use her phone to call a tow company—that had shockingly been able to get his Bronco out, even with the rains. Which was good because leaving it there was a giant hazard.

They were currently waiting on his brothers to come pick them up. But for now they were dry-ish and Flora had been feeding them nonstop. She looked up as the woman stepped into the room, a smile on her face.

"That young man of yours is out there talking to the owner of the tow truck company—one of my nephews. Don't you worry, he'll get you two squared away."

She started to tell the woman that Mac wasn't her "young man" but decided not to. Instead she smiled, beyond grateful for the woman's hospitality. "Thank you...for everything. Especially these sugar cookies." She picked one up and grinned. She'd already eaten five and could eat five more. They were melt-in-her-mouth delicious.

"No problem at all. I'm just sorry y'all got caught in this nasty flooding." Her house phone rang and she shook her head. "Just give me a minute." She disappeared then, somewhere into the house, but Adeline stayed where she was, dry enough and eating.

"You save any of those for me?" Mac's tone was amused as he stepped into the room a minute later. Flecks of rain covered his hair, beard and shirt, but he must have been standing on the front porch because he was just a little wet and it was still coming down outside.

She slid the tin closer to herself and grinned. "All mine."

He snorted as he went to pour a mug of coffee—Flora had made them a fresh pot as well. And maybe it was simply because they'd needed it, but Adeline swore it was the best damn coffee she'd ever had.

Laughing lightly, she unclenched the tin and pushed it across the table as he sat. "Save me from myself and eat these."

He plucked a couple up in one of his very capable, big hands. "How are you doing?"

"Okay. Much better. Sorry about all the crying."

"Don't apologize. Sometimes we all need a good crying jag."

She blinked at him.

Which made him laugh. "It's just something my mom always said. Stuck with me, I guess."

That made more sense because no way in hell could she picture this man having a good crying jag. "So everything is good on your end? With your Bronco?"

"Yeah, they're towing it back to the local shop. They won't attempt to deliver it to Verona Bay until after all this rain. It's not a priority, and I get it. I was able to unload everything so we'll be able to take our stuff home when my brothers get here."

"That's incredible." She felt lucky to be okay right about now.

"Agreed." He ate three cookies and sipped his coffee.

Silence stretched between them, but she could hear Flora in a nearby room, laughing at something whoever she was talking to said.

"So...I told you about my ex," she blurted. Yeah, she'd told him a nightmare of a story. "Now you get to tell me about one of yours." Because she wanted to know a whole lot more about him.

She'd more or less made a decision, or at least it was currently solidifying in her mind.

Mac made a grunting sound.

"Uh-uh. You're telling me something. I'm still feeling off-kilter and need to talk."

"Then we'll talk about something else. Like how you ended up in Verona Bay."

"I threw an arrow at a map of north Florida."

He made a sort of startled sound. "For real?"

"Yep. Now come on."

Now he grumbled a bit but his lips curved up ever so slightly. "I dated some when I was in the Marines, though date is probably a strong word. I had a lot of fun back when I was younger."

She snorted softly, taking a sip of her own coffee, which needed a refreshing pour to heat it up, she realized. "You liked to play the field?" That didn't really line up with the Mac she knew now.

"Eh. I was just a young guy who thought he was hot shit."

"You *are* hot." Oh...oh God. Oh, holy awkward flying pianos. What the hell had she just said?

His blue eyes flared with surprise as he set his cup down with a quiet thud.

Damn it, she needed to say something. What... *Fuuuuck.* What the hell were words? Nothing was coming to mind right now.

"You're hot too. Gorgeous, if I'm being blunt." He watched her intently, spearing her with those eyes she wanted to drown in.

Wait...oh. Warmth spread through her at his words. Well, then. She cleared her throat. "When we get back, if that offer for a date is still open—"

"It is."

She grinned at his quick answer. "Then I'd like to take you up on it." The man was gorgeous, he was attracted to her—and vice versa—made her feel safe, and he was just a good person. After today, she didn't want to live with regrets. She'd once told Serenity that life was too short and she needed to allow herself to be happy. It was about time she took her own advice.

"How about Saturday night? I'll pick you up at six."

"That sounds great." Thunder rumbled, shaking the house slightly, but this time she didn't jump.

She had a date with Mac Collins.

CHAPTER TEN

Mac felt like he was walking on air as he strode up the front steps to his house.

"Why are you grinning like that?" Dylan stared at him as they reached the top of the porch. "I thought you'd be moaning about the loss of your 'child.'"

A clear reference to his Bronco—which Mac didn't let his brothers drive. Ever. "Just happy to be home." And have a date with Adeline.

"Or more likely he's just happy he got to spend time with Adeline," Joe said as he brought up the rear, hurrying to get out of the rain.

Mac ignored his brother, annoyed at his perceptiveness. Or maybe Mac hadn't been that subtle when his brothers had picked them up. He'd expertly moved Joe out of the way when he'd gone to try and sit by Adeline.

"Yeah, what's up with you guys? There was a weird energy in the truck between you two," Dylan said.

"When did you turn into a nosy old lady?" They'd dropped Adeline off, he'd talked to the tow truck company again about delivering his Bronco to a local shop later, and *he had a date with Adeline.* That thought kept playing in his head. As he stepped inside his house, he breathed a sigh of relief. There was something to be said about coming home.

"I notice you're not answering the question," Dylan murmured.

"I don't remember a question," he muttered as he stepped into the kitchen. Sometimes his brothers could be slobs but thankfully the place looked good. Probably because they hadn't cooked for themselves the few days he'd been gone. Either way it was nice not to come home to a disaster area. *God, when had* he *turned into such an old man?*

"Oh, I asked a question." Dylan opened the fridge and grabbed a sports drink.

Mac absently took stock of Dylan. Damn, when had his brother gotten so big? Having just turned twenty-one, he wasn't a kid anymore, that was for sure. But...he looked buff in a way he hadn't before. "You been working out?" he asked Dylan.

Dylan shrugged as he unscrewed the cap. "Come on, answer."

"It's not a crime to be in a good mood." When they both continued staring at him, he frowned. "Fine, yes, I liked spending time with her. We made the best of the...situation." There was no way in hell he could ever call or think of being under the same roof with her as a bad situation. Even with everything that had happened afterward. He'd been concerned about keeping her safe, but even through all that he'd enjoyed being with Adeline.

"Uh-huh. So what was up with that intense hug she gave you? And the covert looks you two kept giving each other?" Joe stood next to Dylan, hands shoved in his pockets. They both stared at him, basically unblinking.

This was bizarre. Normally he was the one asking them about their dating lives—mainly because he didn't have one of his own. But he was their older brother. This... He didn't know if he liked the tables being turned.

"And what was up with the way you practically growled at us for hugging her?" Dylan's eyebrow rose now.

"You two need to find a hobby."

Joe elbowed Dylan and they both grinned at each other simultaneously.

"So you finally made a move, then?" Dylan asked.

Mac paused for a long moment. He was well over a decade-plus older than his brothers. This was definitely a new phase of their relationship. He'd been more of a father figure than a big brother to Dylan and Joe. Sometimes he was both, and the line always got blurred. But his brothers had always been open with him, so he wanted to do the same with them. "We're going out Saturday."

Now they both grinned at him even wider, and though they were roughly a year apart and Dylan was bulkier, they might as well be twins for their maniacal grins.

"And?" Joe pushed.

"And what? That's it." That was all they were getting anyway.

"And where are you taking her? Do you even know what to do on a date anymore?" Joe persisted. "You're kinda rusty, so have you thought about your moves?"

"Yeah," Dylan chimed in. "Shit's changed since the Stone Age."

"I swear to God, we're not having this conversation." He scrubbed a hand over his face. "And I'm not taking advice from a nineteen and just turned twenty-one-year-old."

"Please, I've got more game than both you two," Joe said.

"Hey." Dylan elbowed him.

"You know it's true," Joe said.

Dylan frowned. "So? Don't have to be a dick about it."

Joe rolled his eyes and turned back to Mac, his expression serious. "She likes the Thai place over on Loveless Street. She mentioned it once during a tutoring session. And—"

"You guys, this is one area I so do *not* need help in. Conversation over." This thing between him and Adeline was new, but he wasn't so old that he didn't know what to do with a woman anymore.

"Did you ever get a hold of the sheriff?" Joe asked, taking a hint and changing the subject.

"No." He inwardly cursed. That was on his long-ass list of things to do tomorrow. But it wasn't so late that he couldn't call Lincoln now. "I'll try again," he said, pulling his phone out. Then he stepped out of the kitchen, heading toward the back door.

He flipped on the porch lights before stepping out onto the back patio. The floodlights illuminated everything well past the yard, all the way to the tree line. His parents had never fenced anything in, never had the need to out here in the country. But he frowned as he moved to the edge of the deck. There were unmistakable tire tracks all over the place. Tufts of grass were turned up everywhere and the waterlogged tracks made random crisscross patterns. No way his brothers had done this.

"Joe, Dylan!" he called out before tucking his phone away. He'd already left a voicemail for Lincoln, he wasn't going to leave another. Maybe he'd stop by the station though.

"What's up?" They both stepped out together, Joe in the lead.

"You guys take out the four-wheelers?" He had them locked up in the shed normally and he didn't see them out. And he just couldn't believe they would have jacked up the yard like this.

"We haven't taken anything out. It's been too muddy." Dylan's gaze followed Mac's to the thick tracks leading to the tree line. "What the hell is all this?" Dylan's face darkened and so did Joe's.

"I was out here before we left to pick you up and it wasn't like this," Joe said.

Mac jumped off the back deck and hurried across the wet yard. With all the rain, it would take a while to dry out.

"I can't imagine who this could be." Dylan crouched down next to the tracks at the tree line. "This is weird.

Joe's right, someone must have come by when we were picking you up. But...*where* did they come from?"

"I wonder if it's the same four-wheeler tracks me and Marcy saw," Joe murmured, his muddy boots making a thick popping sound as he took a step closer.

"Y'all get back in the house," Mac said as he pulled his phone out again. He was going to get through to the sheriff no matter what now. Or stop by in person.

"What's going on?" Joe asked.

"Maybe nothing. But no one should be out here on our property like this." Their direct "neighbors" to the left were an elderly couple who were a few miles away. Mac had a bad feeling this was from their other "neighbor" to the south. Harlan Hayward.

He had to tell Lincoln what Joe had seen, and let him know about this. If there was a meth house on the neighboring property, Mac did *not* want to get tangled up with any of those people. Especially if Harlan was involved. He was a real piece of work.

Hayward always had a mean streak. Mac believed that people could change and he sure as hell believed in rehabilitation, but Harlan...his meanness went bone-deep. Something told Mac that prison had only made him worse.

"Come on." He quickly herded his brothers inside. He was going to take care of this one way or another. With or without the sheriff.

CHAPTER ELEVEN

Mac adjusted his backpack higher up as he trekked through the woods. Night had fallen, and once his brothers had gone to bed he'd snuck out. After talking to Lincoln, who'd been frustratingly vague on what he planned to do, Mac was taking things into his own hands. Because when it came to his brothers' safety, all bets were off. Those tire tracks in his yard, whether they'd been a warning or not, he was sure taking them as one. Someone from Harlan's property—likely Harlan himself—had come onto Mac's property for a reason. And leaving his backyard a mess like that? Yeah, that was a message.

So Mac was going to do some recon of his own. Only he wasn't going to leave a bunch of tracks behind.

Years ago he'd been behind enemy lines more times than he wanted to remember. This was very similar, trekking through the woods at night, using the darkness to his advantage.

The moon was half full, which was good and bad. It illuminated the woods in front of him, and now that the rain had finally stopped it was easy enough to move un-hindered.

Following Joe's instructions, he'd found the trailer easily enough. And he'd also found six different trip wires between trees, all of which he'd avoided instead of

101

disabling. The traps were decent but nothing he couldn't handle. There'd been tons of footprints all around where the traps had been set up. Might as well put up a big sign advertising them.

He crouched down next to an oak tree and pulled out his night-vision binoculars. Someone was definitely in the trailer, and Joe had been right. There was extra ventilation, lots of trash, all the windows were open despite the chilly weather—all sorts of signs that this was a meth house. That, combined with the trip wires surrounding the area, left no doubt that this place was bad news.

As he scanned his surroundings, looking for other traps, video surveillance or people, something rumbled in the distance—a vehicle that needed its muffler changed.

Remaining crouched low, he barely moved his binoculars in the direction of the sound. A jacked-up truck rolled up to the trailer, its music blaring. *Morons.*

He pulled out his phone and recorded two men jumping out of the vehicle, laughing and stumbling as they headed for the front door.

Before they reached it, the front door to the trailer swung open and a man he didn't recognize stepped out with a mask shoved up on his head. Mac looked through the binos, could see how angry the man was—until it was clear he recognized the men.

"Hey fuckers, what are y'all doing here?" His tone was lighthearted as he hurried down the rickety wooden steps.

"You need a break and we need some fun. Let's head up to the Lucky Lady for a couple hours," one of the guys said. "It's two for one on drinks tonight."

The Lucky Lady was a strip club the next town over. Next, there was some back and forth, some shit-talking, and then the man from the trailer finally nodded and pulled his mask fully off and jumped in the back of the truck with the two rednecks. Mac didn't recognize the guy, but he memorized his face.

He waited a solid five minutes after they were gone, wondering if the place was completely empty now. There'd been no other movement inside other than the lightly blowing curtains, but it looked as if that was because of a fan.

First he made sure his balaclava was fully in place, then he checked his backpack. He had everything he might need. And a chance like this might not present itself again. Someone had come to his house, onto his property. Mac wasn't waiting for Lincoln to take care of this.

He hurried down the slight slope from the woods, staying low until he reached the "yard" around the trailer. That was when he realized the door to the trailer hadn't even been shut properly. These guys really were careless—but that didn't mean they weren't dangerous.

Before reaching the stairs, he tugged his half-respirator mask on over his balaclava. No way was he breathing in whatever shit was in there. Luckily he had plenty of masks he used when working with different stains and paints. That wasn't the only protection he had either—he pulled his pistol out as well.

Bypassing the jagged nail on one of the broken steps, he paused when he saw the small video camera pointed down at the door. Too late to stop now. A light didn't go off so he couldn't tell if it was live or not. At least his balaclava completely hid his beard and most of his face. Weapon up, he eased inside and automatically swept the trashed living room, looking for danger. Open to-go containers were piled up next to the brown and orange couch. What looked like rat shit was littered around the containers. *Ugh.* He was extra glad for his mask as he stepped farther inside. How did people exist like this?

The nearest bedroom was where the production area was. He didn't step all the way inside, but took pictures instead.

As he did, the same rumble as before filled the air.

Shit. They were back.

Heart racing, he pocketed his phone and hurried back to the front of the trailer, to laughter and... Gunshots.

"Told you I could hit that bottle." Another gunshot, then maniacal laughter.

"And I told you I want to go to the Lucky Lady!"

"I'm not paying for some pussy to dance up on me."

Mac peered out one of the windows, easing the soiled curtain back. It was the same three guys from before shooting at empty bottles set up along a fence line. No way in hell could he sneak out the front door now.

They'd clearly see him. And even if he jumped out the back window, there was no guarantee he'd get away without being seen.

He quickly weighed his options, then went with the one that would have the loudest boom—and be the biggest distraction. He simply couldn't risk being seen by these guys.

Not to mention it would get rid of one of his problems.

Reaching into his backpack, he pulled out a grenade with gloved hands.

Hurrying back through the disgusting trailer, he moved into what turned out to be a makeshift bedroom filled with product and a mattress with stains he didn't want to think about.

Luckily the window was already open so he hoisted himself up and through it. Still hearing laughter—so he knew the three men were still outside—he pulled the pin, tossed the grenade back inside, and hauled ass.

His legs burning as he ran, the blast rent through the air with a thunderous boom.

Heat and the concussion punched through the air, rippling at his back, but he didn't turn around.

He had a head start and the three guys were on the other side of the trailer with no visibility of him. Chances of them seeing him or realizing what'd happened were almost nil at this point. They would assume shit had gone wrong with their production, that something had detonated and destroyed everything. And they'd be grateful to be alive.

That was what Mac was banking on anyway as he sprinted toward the edge of the woods. Once he was past the line of trees, he paused and crouched, whipping his binoculars out again.

Flames licked across the demolished trailer but he could make out... Yep, three men. They were talking over one another, and one appeared to be on his phone.

Mac wondered who he was calling—likely whoever was in charge. A sliver of regret settled in his gut. If they figured out what he'd done, he'd officially made himself and his family a target.

He'd deal with that later. For now, he had to get out of here.

* * *

Mac quietly opened his back door, stepping into the kitchen, but immediately froze.

He wasn't alone.

Suddenly the light flipped on. Both Dylan and Joe were at the kitchen table, watching him with matching accusing expressions.

"What are you guys doing? It's after midnight."

"I think the real question is, what are you doing dressed like a ninja sneaking back into the house?" Dylan demanded.

"I'm not sneaking anywhere." Okay, he had been. "And I didn't realize I needed to check in with you two before going out."

"Is that a balaclava?" Dylan nodded at the mask Mac had tucked into the side pocket of his backpack.

"And why are you wearing gloves?" Joe demanded.

"It's cold outside." Okay, he sounded like a petulant teenager at this point.

Both of his brothers simply stared at him. Always the spokesperson of the two, Joe spoke first. "We're adults now. And you always made it clear that we had equal voices in this house. You're more than just a brother to us and we care about you. We care about what's going on in your life. Are you in trouble?"

They both stepped toward him, almost as if they had choreographed it. And their matching expressions of concern made him feel like a dick. He knew they weren't kids anymore, but they were still his responsibility. And...he did need to tell them what was going on.

He tugged his gloves off and moved to the sink. He tossed them and his backpack onto the countertop before soaping up his hands. He wanted to burn everything he'd been wearing after being in that shithole. "I'm not in trouble. Or I don't think I am. I went to scout out that meth house you told me about." Grabbing a dish towel, he started drying his hands as he turned to look at them again.

"By yourself?" Dylan demanded, his big arms crossed over his chest.

"You should have taken us," Joe added.

"You guys don't have the experience to do the recon, and there's no way I'm putting you in danger."

"But putting yourself in danger is okay?" Joe countered.

"I have training. You don't. Unfortunately, things sort of got out of hand. Not intentionally." He cleared his throat. He didn't want to explain everything, but he needed to tell them what had happened. "I accidentally had to blow up the trailer. With a grenade." And had probably destroyed all usable evidence in the process.

His brothers' eyes widened.

"Wait, you accidentally did, or you *had* to?" Dylan asked. "And how the hell did you have a grenade?"

"Technically it wasn't an accident. I *did* bring the grenade with me," he muttered. "I just didn't plan to use it. And...you don't need to know how I had it." It was a souvenir of sorts from a long-ago mission. A life that felt like it hadn't even been his sometimes. Right after his parents had died and he'd been tasked with guardianship of his brothers, everything had changed in an instant. He hadn't planned to get out of the Marines but he also wasn't letting someone else raise his brothers. A friend had given it to him at his "returning to civilian life" party, as they'd called it. He shouldn't have kept it, but that didn't matter now.

"Did anyone see you?" Joe asked.

"No. Or I'm pretty sure no. But...we need to be careful. That property is owned by Chief Hayward." Or it had been at one time, and Mac assumed it still was. "I wore a mask and gloves, and the trailer is demolished now so there's no way they could find any DNA. Not that I think they have the capability to scour for DNA anyway, but

still. No one saw my face. No one even saw me at all."
Unless that camera had recorded something and saved it
to the cloud. It hadn't looked very high-tech, however.

He'd watched the men from the woods for a little
while and they'd been more concerned about the fire
than anything else. They hadn't shouted or acted as if
they'd seen him. He *should* be fine. Still, worry tingled in
the back of his neck. He'd put his brothers in danger because of his actions. Put himself in danger. And...if Harlan figured out it had been him who'd blown up his meth
lab...Mac had just put *everyone* in his life in danger.

If he started dating Adeline, that would mean putting her in danger too.

Ah, hell.

He scrubbed both hands over his face. He would
have to cancel their date tomorrow night. He just... He
really didn't want to. But no way in hell was he going to
inadvertently put her in danger because of him. He
shoved that thought away for now.

"So what does this mean?" Joe asked.

"I can't call the cops and tell them what I did. But I
think we need to be prepared that if Harlan or his dad
figure out it was me, they'll come after us." Some guardian he'd turned out to be. *Damn it.*

"We're done with the interior of the house on Mel-
ody Drive," Dylan said, referring to the two-bedroom,
two bath they'd bought with the intention of flipping. It
had been a side project for all of them, one they'd been
working on for the last eight months in between jobs,
life and his brothers' classes. They'd decided to rent it out

instead of selling it. There were still a few finishing touches to be done before they could do that, however. For now, it would make a good place to lie low.

"Okay, then that's our base. If something happens, if you think you're being followed, if someone shows up here, whatever. If there's any danger, you call the sheriff department and *that's* where you go. Just make sure you're not followed."

His brothers nodded in agreement.

"When does Marcy get back?" Mac asked Joe. His girlfriend had just gone out of town with her parents for the holidays.

"Two weeks."

That was something at least. "Closer to her return, if necessary, we'll let her know that she needs to be careful. But let's cross that bridge when we get to it." He was hoping that Lincoln would be able to arrest these guys before then.

Unfortunately, he had to cancel his date with Adeline. She couldn't have any link to him. Not if he'd just made himself a target.

CHAPTER TWELVE

Lincoln looked up as Marisol Machado, one of his newest deputies, stepped into his office.

Her dark hair was pulled back in a bun against her neck and lines of tension bracketed her mouth. "You wanted to see me?"

"Yeah, and can you shut the door? And maybe don't look so nervous," he said lightly.

She let out a laugh as she shut the door behind her. Then she stood at attention in front of his desk, her fingers linked together.

"You can sit."

She did but her shoulders were still bunched tight. He wondered why she was so nervous.

"I need to talk to you about something and I want to keep it between us. At least right now." After hearing from Mac about a potential meth house on the Hayward property and the tire tracks all over Mac's yard, Lincoln had already started the process of getting a search warrant. It just took time.

She frowned but nodded. "What's up?"

"What do you think about Chief Hayward? I want your honest opinion." Marisol had worked with the Harrison Police Department a while ago. Then she'd moved to Miami for about a year before applying with him at the sheriff's department in Verona Bay. She was his newest hire, having been with them for six months, and she was definitely going to be a detective sooner than later. She was smart, and cared about the town.

She blinked, the tension in her shoulders easing. "That's what you wanted to talk about?"

"Yeah, what did you think?"

"Nothing," she said quickly. Then she cleared her throat. "Hayward's a jackass, if I may speak freely."

"*Yes.* Please be as honest as possible. I've got my own impressions and I've heard some things over the years but I want the opinion of someone who worked with him. What was it like working for him?"

She leaned back slightly in her chair and he could tell she was weighing her words. Finally she spoke. "Off the record, he does favors for his friends. Anyone he hunts with, they get a pass for…traffic tickets, whatever. Nothing obscene, but little stuff, yeah. No tickets. The good shifts all go to his favorites and it's not based on seniority—or skill. There's a lot more, little stuff that all adds up. It's definitely a good old boys club at the PD."

Lincoln stiffened slightly. Maybe that was the reason she'd been nervous when he'd asked her into his office. "Is that why you left?" She'd been with the Harrison Police Department for a year before moving to Miami, but then she'd recently moved back to take care of her mom. Lincoln had scooped her up immediately when she'd applied, but he had thought it was interesting she hadn't gone back to the PD.

"Yeah. It's not the only reason, but if I hadn't gotten another job down in Miami, I would have left eventually. As a woman in law enforcement, I'm used to dealing with sexist bullshit, but it was next-level with Hayward. He would call me in to his office to tell me stupid jokes. Real sexist shit, you know? It was like he was trying to get under my skin just for the sake of it."

Lincoln clenched his jaw. The more he found out about Hayward, the more he was determined to get this guy out of law enforcement. "Does he ever do anything...illegal?"

She lifted a shoulder. "I don't know. I literally kept my head down, tried to do my job well and was biding my time until I could get out of there. There's no ill will between us or anything. I don't think he knows how much I despise him. There were rumors of him looking the other way for petty stuff, but since moving back I heard that his son just got out of jail. I guess he got into some bad stuff years ago? I don't really know the details. And honestly, I don't really care. If it wasn't for my mom refusing to move to Verona Bay, I wouldn't even be living over in Harrison."

He nodded, tapping his finger against his desk. "How would you feel about doing some low-key stakeouts involving him?"

"Oh yeah," she blurted. She cleared her throat. "I mean, that sounds good."

"I like the enthusiasm." He tapped his finger again. "We've got a tip that there might be some illegal activity on a property he recently gave to his son—a meth house.

It borders our jurisdiction but it's not actually *in* our jurisdiction. I've talked to a judge about getting a warrant to do surveillance and we should be good to go soon."

She nodded. "Just tell me what you need me to do."

"I will. I know I said that this stays between us and I'm just reiterating that. That means you can't tell anyone, not even your mom."

"I get it."

He leaned back in his chair. He likely didn't even need to reiterate with her, but he didn't want anything to go wrong. Surveilling the neighboring chief of police was a big deal. "I'll probably bring a couple others into this but I wanted to get your honest take on him first, since you worked for him."

Nodding, she stood. "I won't say a word to anyone. And if he is involved with meth, I hope we nail the bastard."

He grinned. "Me too."

CHAPTER THIRTEEN

Adeline turned away from the mirror, tired of looking at herself. The more she did, the more critical she got, and it was exhausting. "Does this look like I'm trying too hard?"

"Who cares if it looks like you're trying?" Bianca said. "You look stunning. Mac is going to be eating his heart out. And maybe you, if you're lucky."

She let out a burst of laughter. "Believe me, I've had a lot of fantasies about that man. I think he's a giver." She'd definitely wondered how his beard would feel against the juncture of her thighs if he went down on her. *Whew.* She had to cut off that thought before she got all flustered.

Bianca made a sound of agreement.

Adeline turned back to the mirror, eyeing the V-neck of her sweater dress. It was light enough for Florida winter, and paired with the knee-high boots... Okay, she *did* look stunning. She'd added a long silver necklace that sat right between her breasts, and damn, her cleavage was rocking tonight. The last time he'd seen her she'd looked like a drowned rat, soaked and just happy to be alive. Not that he'd seemed to care at all. When he looked at her, it was like he just wanted to consume her. While Adeline wasn't sure exactly what she was ready for with

Mac, she knew she didn't want to live her life on the sidelines anymore.

"I'm nervous," she admitted as she went to her dresser and put a pair of big, sparkly hoops in her ears.

"I get it, it's been forever since you've been on a date. Actually, have you ever dated anyone in Verona Bay?" Bianca, sitting in the club chair by the window in Adeline's bedroom, took a sip of her wine.

"No. And I'm too embarrassed to tell you how long it's been since before moving here."

"Well you're not the only one with a date this weekend—though mine is tomorrow."

She turned from her dresser, surprised Bianca was only now telling her. "Who?"

"The new teacher at the high school."

"Oh, she's gorgeous. And she seems so nice." She brought her Maltese in to the dog grooming shop every couple weeks. "Did you ask her out or did she ask you out?"

"She's been coming to the shop every afternoon for months and I finally worked up the courage to ask her out. She said she was close to asking me out too. Apparently we're both shy nerds."

"I know it's way too soon but I'm already planning on double dates in our future." Gah, she couldn't get ahead of herself but for the first time in years Adeline could admit that she was beyond excited about a man. Mac was the kind of man you simply didn't let go of. She'd opened up to him, told him things about herself she'd only told a select few. And he'd been so damn wonderful and steady about it all.

"Me too! Oh God, I really am a nerd." She groaned and took another sip of her wine.

Adeline glanced down at her phone and her heart skipped a beat when she saw Mac's name flash onscreen. He was supposed to pick her up in an hour and she was already ready because yes, she was that excited.

Her stomach twisted, however, when she saw the message on the screen. What the hell?

"What is it?" She was aware of Bianca setting her wineglass down and standing.

Feeling numb, Adeline held out her phone.

"I need to cancel tonight. And I don't think we should go out in the future," Bianca read aloud. Then she growled. "What a bastard! And what a shitty way to blow you off."

"I can't believe he blew me off through text. Actually, I can't believe he's blowing me off at all. Not because I think I'm so hot, but... The chemistry between us has been insane. And he's the one who pursued me, asking me out more than once." And they'd had a connection, one she knew wasn't one-sided. She grabbed her phone back and stared at the message. Instead of responding the way she wanted to, she set her phone down and then collapsed on the club chair.

She wasn't going to respond at all. Not yet anyway. Tears burned the back of her eyes but she blinked them back as anger and hurt swelled to the surface, warring for domination.

"I want to go toilet-paper his precious Bronco."

Adeline let out a startled laugh at the venom in Bianca's tone. "We're not going to do anything. Besides, he had to have it towed. He likely doesn't even have it back yet." A heavy weight settled on her chest and she realized…it was pain. An ache had started and was spreading. She'd felt safe enough to open up to Mac, to confess something hard to him and…this was what he did?

"A text," Bianca muttered as she went back to grab her wine. "A freaking text."

Adeline started taking her earrings out but Bianca shook her head.

"No way. Put those back in. We're going out."

"I don't feel like it." Her throat burned with unshed tears, but she wasn't going to break down over something she'd never had anyway. It just… Damn, it hurt. Plain and simple.

"We're not going drinking or anything, but we're going to get pie and coffee."

She stood even as tightness settled in her chest at the way he'd so casually dismissed her after everything they'd been through. She thought they'd bonded, that she'd meant something to him.

Bianca was right. She wasn't going to let him ruin her night. Which was pretty much a lie, because he had *definitely* ruined it, but she'd dressed up, and screw him. Pie sounded amazing. "Fair warning, I'm probably going to eat an entire pie."

"I'm going to ban him from my shop," Bianca said as she picked up her purse.

"No you're not," she muttered, grabbing her own clutch.

"Oh, we'll see. Maybe I won't ban him, but he's getting day-old coffee and none of the good croissants he likes. I'm always going to be sold out of whatever he wants when he's in there."

"You're ridiculous."

"And he's a jackass."

Despite the ache in her chest, a small smile touched her lips at her friend's loyalty. "You're a good friend, thanks."

And Mac wasn't the man Adeline had thought he was. No, he was just another asshole.

CHAPTER FOURTEEN

"I really love your quilt top," Serenity said to Adeline as she, Bianca, and a handful of others walked to their cars. "I'm probably going to copy you and make the same thing next."

They now met on Thursdays instead of Tuesdays for their quilting group, and much to Adeline's delight, Norah—who'd been a bit of a nightmare—had sold her shop to someone else, and they all really liked the new owner, Virginia Campbell. In her forties, a widow with two kids under the age of ten, she seemed to have never-ending energy and had come up with so many different ideas for the shop—which was now called Next-Level Stitch.

And the place had a more modern feel, catering to both the older and younger quilting generations. They even had two men in their group, which Adeline loved. The more people who quilted, the better.

"Thanks," she said, hoping she sounded cheerful enough. She'd gone with a chevron pattern of teals, grays and whites. It was definitely more on the modern end of quilts and she planned to give it to Serenity as a gift, so she was glad her best friend liked it so much.

Even after a fun quilting class with friends, she was still reeling over Mac's rejection Saturday night. Maybe she was overreacting but she still was stunned. He'd just ripped the rug right out from underneath her. And she wasn't working, since she was still on her vacation. It had given her a lot of time to paint angrily—and she'd had too much time with her thoughts. She'd been so tempted to respond to his text, but everything she came up with was too ragey. And the thought of sending a rude message made *her* feel bad, so nope, she wasn't doing that.

"I really love what both of you guys are doing," she said. "Especially the little fox quilt you're making for Autumn. It's too cute for words."

Serenity grinned. "I know it's not a competition or anything, but I'm hoping it's the best baby gift she gets at her shower."

Adeline snickered even as Bianca shook her head and unloaded her sewing machine into the back of her car. The new LED lights in the parking lot were bright and lit the whole area up like a Christmas tree. After everything that had happened a year ago, Adeline was glad for the extra security measures. It made walking to her car at night a whole lot less stressful.

Adeline said goodbye to Serenity then set her own sewing machine in the back of her rental car. She liked the rental but was looking forward to getting her car back. The roads were mostly clear now and she'd been assured by the towing company that she should have it in two days.

"So have you heard from the jackass?" Bianca said as she came to stand next to the back of Adeline's car.

"No," she grumbled. And Bianca was the only one who knew about the planned date with Mac and what had happened. Normally she would have told Serenity—they were business partners and best friends—but Serenity had so much on her plate these weeks leading up to Christmas that Adeline didn't want to add to it.

And...she didn't want all her friends feeling sorry for her. It was the holidays and she was trying really hard not to let a dark mood suck her under. The holidays were always a bit hard for her, and then this on top of it? She really needed to paint something else. Dark and ragey. Rage-painting? That totally had to be a thing.

"Speaking of jackasses." Bianca's eyes narrowed as she looked over Adeline's shoulder at something.

Adeline knew who rather than what Bianca was looking at before she turned. Against her will, she glanced over her shoulder to see Joe, Mac, and a blonde-haired woman she didn't recognize walking down the sidewalk across the street.

When Joe saw her, he waved and smiled. "Hey, Adeline!"

She winced again because she couldn't very well ignore him. She adored Joe. She waved back, smiling at him. Mac's gaze locked on her and she gave him an obnoxious wave. Or maybe not obnoxious, but her smile felt super fake. Baring her teeth at him would be wrong, right? Yeah, totally wrong. So she kept waving.

And he didn't even wave back.

Gritting her teeth, she whipped around. "We definitely need to go get pie again. Right *now.*"

Bianca lifted an eyebrow. "Pie, or a carton of eggs."

She frowned. "Eggs?"

"You know, to egg his truck. It's dark out, we won't get caught."

Laughter escaped even though she was holding on to her anger really well. "What are we, thirteen?"

"I was just kidding. Unless you said yes, then I would totally be in to egg his Bronco, but yeah, *totally* joking."

"I'm eating a whole pie." And ice cream.

"Good, then I won't feel so bad for doing the same." Bianca linked arms with Adeline as the cold breeze rolled over them, rustling her curls. "Come on, we can walk from here."

Her boots clicked along the sidewalk as they headed in the opposite direction, and no way in hell was she turning around to see if she could still spot Mac. Even if she wanted a glimpse of him. Even if she *really* wanted to smack that hard look off his face.

Seriously, what was wrong with him? It was like he'd turned into a different person. Cold and distant.

Nothing like the man she'd spent time with at the cabin. She was probably better off without him anyway, knowing he could just flip a switch like that.

* * *

"Thanks for walking me to my car," Evelyn said as they reached her Mini Cooper on Main Street.

Mac nodded and glanced behind them, hoping for a peek of Adeline. Even if he knew he had to keep his distance, he still craved seeing her. Tonight she'd been in jeans and a sparkly Christmas sweater.

"No problem, see you later," Joe said as he and Mac continued down the sidewalk.

They'd walked her to her car when she'd gotten off work at the ice cream shop. She and Joe had gone to school together, and she hadn't wanted to walk alone. Or that was what she'd said anyway. She'd been a little flirty with Joe but his brother hadn't seemed to notice. Or maybe he hadn't cared. No, Joe was over the moon for Marcy and didn't see anyone else. Something Mac understood.

"What was up with that?"

Mac shrugged. Maybe his little brother *had* noticed. "I don't know, I guess she likes you," he said absently, glancing behind him again. He needed to keep his head on straight, not strain for a peek of Adeline when he knew she was long gone. But here he was, doing just that like a dumbass. Nothing had come of the other night after he'd blown up that trailer, but that didn't mean things were over. He hadn't heard anything from Lincoln either, which was just frustrating.

"Huh? What are you talking about? What was up with you ignoring Adeline when she waved to you? You stood there like a total dick."

Ah. Jaw tight, Mac faced forward, pressed the key fob to Dylan's truck—his brother had let him borrow it since he still didn't have his Bronco back. And that was making him cranky too. "Mind your business."

"Hell no. All the years I've had to listen to you talk about how to treat a woman—and you are one hundred percent right—so you're not getting out of this. What's going on with you? Adeline is like the nicest person in the world. Seriously, she helped pull me out of freezing cold waters, was crazy patient while tutoring me. And I know you like her. So what's up?"

"I don't want to talk about it." He started the engine, careful of his surroundings. It didn't matter that he hadn't had any problems with Harlan, he knew the man wasn't going to announce his intent to come after Mac if he decided to.

"Come on, man."

He fought for patience. "We were supposed to go out, but with what happened...I canceled on her. If Harlan figures out what I did, I don't want to make her a target." And he'd waited until the last minute like a total ass. He'd gone back and forth in his head, trying to convince himself that it would be okay if he took her out. But in the end he'd known he couldn't be that selfish, couldn't put her in danger.

"Oh...shit. That sucks." Joe slumped against the passenger seat. "You two would be good together. Maybe if you just explained to her—"

"Just let it go."

He wasn't going to explain anything to her, wasn't going to bring any danger to her life. That was the last thing he would ever do to Adeline Rodriguez. He *cared* about her, more than he even wanted to acknowledge to himself. He wouldn't put anyone in danger intentionally, but her? Hell no.

The drive home was tense, or maybe he was just projecting his own emotions. But as his headlights flashed across the driveway, he stopped the truck. "You see that?"

"See what?" Joe looked up from his phone where he'd been busy texting, likely with Marcy.

Mac inwardly cursed. "Sit tight. I thought I saw movement along the side of the house."

Joe shoved his phone away and unstrapped. "What are you going to do?"

"Just stay here." He pulled his pistol out from under the seat. Normally he didn't drive around with a weapon, but after what he'd done he didn't want to be caught unawares if Harlan decided to attack him. He killed the lights but kept the truck running. "If you have to run, get out of here and call the sheriff." It could have been a deer or rabbit. The movement had been so damn slight and fast.

He slipped out of the vehicle, ignoring Joe's protests as he shut the door behind him. His eyes adjusted quickly to the darkness, the solar lights he had around the property in the front yard giving him enough illumination. Not to mention he knew this place inside and out. He moved to the edge of the house, held his weapon up and flipped on his flashlight.

Then he swept along the yard— There!

A figure wearing a hoodie raced across the backyard.

He cursed, ran along the side of the house, but slowed as the figure disappeared into the tree line.

As he reached the edge of the back wall, he flipped on his flashlight, looking for another intruder behind the house or in the backyard. Ice coated his veins at what he saw.

A gas can sat on the back patio. With a gloved hand, he picked it up. It was still full at least, and it didn't smell as if someone had doused the back patio.

He felt his phone buzz in his pocket, but ignored it. *Hell.* This had escalated quickly. Or maybe not. He'd blown up their meth house. Harlan would want revenge.

He knew Dylan was out for the evening with friends so he hurried back to the truck and jumped inside. Then he immediately called the sheriff. There were some things he could handle and some things he could not. Right now, he needed law enforcement.

Once he was done telling Lincoln what he'd found, he looked at Joe. "I want you to get in your car and head to the rental place. If there's anything you need inside, let's grab it quick. I think I scared off whoever that was, but we need to get out of here." He didn't know how much manpower Harlan had, and he wasn't putting Joe in danger.

He knew that leaving now before the sheriff's deputies showed up was a risk, because someone could come back and burn his house down, but if Harlan had a bunch of his guys with him, Mac wasn't going to risk going up against him.

"What are you going to do?"

"Pack a bag myself, then I've gotta stop by my shop." There were a few things he needed to grab, especially if they were going to be hunkering down at the rental for a while.

"What about the sheriff?"

"He said he's sending his deputies out here. I've got to pick up a couple important things from the shop." And he was worried Harlan might go there next. If he hadn't already. He opened the garage and they hurried inside. "After we pack up, you're going to follow me to Rampart Street. Then take a very long way to the rental. Make sure you're not followed."

"I know what to do." Joe sounded exasperated as he opened the door.

"I know you do. Look, I just care about you. I'm your older brother and I get to worry about you. It's my right."

Joe half-smiled. "Okay."

In that moment, Mac knew he'd made the smart choice by blowing off Adeline. At least she wasn't involved in this. At least she had no link to him and was safe.

Harlan would never realize that she meant far too much to him. She would never be a target. Knowing that she was safe, he could focus solely on keeping his family the same.

CHAPTER FIFTEEN

As Adeline headed home, she told herself *not* to do what her brain was trying to convince her to do.

Namely, turn left at Hudson Street, and… She was turning left.

She was going to blame it on the pie. She'd had a slice of blueberry and then a mixed berry slice, both with whipped cream topping. And what had originally been just a spark of anger simmering inside her was now a full-fledged bonfire.

The more she thought about the way Mac had blown her off, the angrier she got. She hadn't been on a date in ages, and she'd finally let her guard down with him. More than that, even.

If he'd changed his mind about dating, fine. But texting her and then just ignoring her in public? She'd done absolutely nothing to deserve that. And yes, she knew she should just let this go. But she wanted to ask him why. Maybe—probably—it was a bad idea, but at the moment she didn't care.

As she made her way to his shop she inwardly cursed. It was getting late and he was probably at home. And she wasn't actually going to go by his house so… Wait, she could see part of a truck parked out back. Not his Bronco, but she recognized it as Dylan's.

And there were lights on inside. Okay, so someone was there. That someone better be Mac, because he was going to listen to her.

Her mom had always warned her that her temper would get her into trouble, but she was justified right now.

The tires of her rental kicked up gravel as she jerked to a stop in the parking lot right by the front door.

With shaking hands, she slung her purse strap over her shoulder, palmed her keys and slammed the door behind her.

She tried the front door and it was unlocked, which actually surprised her.

"Not open," Mac's deep, rumbly voice called out from the back about a second before he stepped out from his workshop. His eyes widened when he saw her.

And he stood there looking like a deer in headlights. Good.

"Adeline," he began.

"A text? Seriously? You blow me off with a freaking text," she snapped out, her boots stomping forward of their own volition. That burning fire that had spent days kindling was licking up her spine now as she worked up a good head of anger.

He closed his eyes briefly as he moved toward her. "Look, it's not what you think."

"*Really?* It's not what I think? You didn't send me a dismissive, crappy text about an hour before our date? After spending all that time together and becoming...friends." Or she'd thought they had. Obviously she was wrong. "So you didn't blow me off after all that? And then ignore me right in front of people on Main Street?" It was quite literally possible there was actual steam coming out of her ears right now.

Guilt flickered across his expression for a moment but then his face went carefully neutral. "Look, I didn't know how else to handle it. I just don't think we should see each other. I shouldn't have ignored you and I should have called, but—"

She'd taken another step forward, hands on hips, when the front door behind her swung open with a bang.

She jumped and turned to find some guy stalking in. He had on heavy-looking boots, jeans, a short-sleeved T-shirt, and there was a chain hanging from his back pocket attached to his belt. And he had some ugly-looking tattoos on his arms. Prison tats. Her ex had worked with people who'd been in prison and she recognized some of the styles.

On instinct she took a step closer to Mac. At the same time he practically shoved her behind him. She peered around him slightly to get a good look at the guy, but mostly stayed hidden behind Mac. A bit of panic buzzed through her. This guy...was bad news. Her radar was pinging like crazy and Mac very clearly didn't want her near the guy.

"What are you doing here?" Mac snarled in a dark tone she'd never heard before from him.

"Stopped by to say hi to an old friend. And who is this pretty piece with you? Does she belong to someone else too?" The man's face went a mottled red as he raised his voice.

"She's just a customer." His tone was stone-cold.

The man laughed, the sound sort of maniacal. "You said that a little too fast for me to believe you."

"Get the hell out of here," Mac said as he urgently started pushing her in the opposite direction.

Fear clawed at her now instead of anger. Mac was trying to push her toward his office. Instinct told her to listen. Her boots made little clicking sounds as she stepped backward, one step after the other, Mac slowly following in her wake. But he never turned his back to the other man. His shoulders were pulled taut and all his muscles practically vibrated as if he was gearing up for a fight.

"I'm not going anywhere," the man spat. "You and I are going to have it out right here and right now, and then I'm gonna have some fun with your girl."

Panic rolled through her at his ugly words. Before she could even think about pulling her phone out to call the sheriff, Mac moved superhumanly fast. He grabbed her, hauling her through the open workshop door and slamming it shut behind him with his boot.

Before she was even steady on her feet, he threw the lock into place.

"You're coming with me," he snapped out, dragging her by the arm to the back door, quickly maneuvering around all the heavy machinery and grabbing a duffel bag as he moved.

Pop. Pop. Pop.

Oh God! She jumped, panic skittering through her as loud bangs slammed into the door.

"It's reinforced but the walls sure aren't," he snapped out, racing to the other door, still holding on to her.

Adeline didn't need him to drag her anymore, she started running with him. He threw the back door open and they both raced to the waiting truck.

More sounds of gunfire from the front erupted and the kind of raw fear that she'd only experienced once before spiraled out of control as she dove into the passenger seat.

Mac had already started the truck before she shut the door, and kicked it into reverse. Her heart raced in her chest as he roared out of the parking lot and tore around the side of the building.

Instead of heading toward the front he made a sharp right across the neighboring parking lot of a feed store. His tires squealed as he zoomed away, and even though she was terrified, she looked behind them to see three men jumping into a pickup truck in the front parking lot.

Her heart rate kicked up even more and she belatedly scrambled to strap in.

"Hang tight," he growled.

"They're not pulling out of the parking lot," she said as he took a left at the stop sign. The truck disappeared from her sight, but she'd seen them just idling.

"This is exactly what I didn't want to happen," he muttered, more to himself than at her as he pulled out his cell phone.

"Who the hell was that?"

Instead of answering her, he called someone—Joe, she realized as she saw his name on the screen.

She gritted her teeth and glanced over her shoulder again. She still didn't see the truck following them, which was a good thing. But her panic hadn't subsided.

Then Mac took a right at the next four-way. Maybe those guys wouldn't catch up to them. "Shouldn't we call the sheriff?" She knew Lincoln would help immediately.

"Hey, are you both at the rental?" Mac said to Joe, ignoring her. There was a pause and then, "Okay, sit tight. I'll see you in ten." Then he hung up.

"Mac!"

"Sorry, I had to make sure my brothers were safe."

"What the hell are you involved in? And *are* your brothers okay?"

"They're fine. And it's sort of a long story."

She glanced through the rearview again and frowned. "Mac…I see smoke back there."

He cursed. "He probably set my place on fire. What were you driving?"

"A rental car."

"Did you have any personal information in there?"

"I don't know. Maybe the paperwork I signed when I picked it up?" She couldn't remember if she'd brought it into her house.

He cursed. "He's seen you now. You're coming with me regardless."

She didn't know what to say as fear clawed at her throat. What the hell had she walked into? Was *this* why he'd blown her off before? To protect her? Before she could ask another question, he called Lincoln—Sheriff Jordan.

Oh, this was very, very bad.

CHAPTER SIXTEEN

Mac pulled into the rental's garage, worried because he didn't see Joe's vehicle out front. But as soon as he and Adeline stepped into the kitchen, both Dylan and Joe were waiting, expressions anxious.

They both stepped forward, and to Mac's surprise, they pulled Adeline into a hug.

She hugged them back tight and patted their shoulders as if they were kids. "Are you guys okay?"

"We're good. What happened with you guys?" They both looked at Mac expectantly.

"The sheriff's on the way over here," he said instead of answering. He didn't want to have to do this more than once.

There was a sharp knock on the front door and they all froze but Mac moved into action first.

"All of you stay here." He glanced through the peephole and saw that it was Lincoln. At least he wasn't in full uniform. This place was supposed to be their safe haven.

He opened the door and looked past Lincoln, saw that there was no car in the driveway.

"I had someone drop me off," Lincoln said tersely as he walked right in.

Not wanting any of the neighbors to notice the sheriff here, Mac stepped back and closed the door.

"What's going on?" Lincoln demanded as Adeline and his brothers met them in the foyer. "I've got the fire department at your shop, Mac. And I've got one of my deputies stationed at both your houses. You were supposed to wait at your house after you called." He frowned.

"Mine too?" Adeline said, surprised.

The sheriff looked at her like she was crazy as he nodded. "Of course."

Mac knew that Lincoln would take precautions for any citizen no matter what, but Adeline was also Lincoln's soon-to-be sister-in-law's business partner and best friend. Plus everyone loved Adeline. It was impossible not to. She was sweet, giving...and he did not need to go down that path. He'd dragged her into this shit and had been mentally berating himself ever since.

"Let's take this into the living room." Mac nodded at the small room right off the entranceway. In here he could stand by the window and keep an eye out on the street. Harlan shouldn't know about this place, but Mac wasn't taking any chances.

"You guys own this house?" Lincoln stood by one of the windows as well, easing one of the blinds back slightly.

"Yeah. It's not in our names though. We set up a small LLC business last year. We were planning to flip it and split the profits but we decided to rent it out instead." Mac noticed that Joe and Dylan had sat on either side of Adeline, as if they were protecting her.

In that moment he was a proud big brother. They'd both turned into good young men. It was hard not to be proud.

"Talk, Mac. I need all the details of whatever is going on." Lincoln stepped away from the window and moved toward a club chair they'd picked up at a consignment shop.

Mac realized why the sheriff had moved. Now Lincoln had a good view of two other windows. Some of his own tension eased at that, but he still remained where he was.

"Harlan Hayward and I go way back." He'd already told Lincoln who'd attacked him and Adeline at his shop—and who he suspected of attempting to set fire to his house earlier. "About seventeen years ago, I guess. I haven't thought of the guy in well over a decade. Longer. Fifteen years, I guess. But when I was eighteen," he said, clearing his throat, "we didn't exactly run in the same crowd but we were sort of adjacent."

"I remember. He's older than me, but he was a bad egg," Lincoln said.

Mac couldn't remember Lincoln ever running wild. He was just one of those stand-up guys who'd always walked a good path. Or at least it seemed that way.

"I hooked up with his on-again, off-again girlfriend when they were off one time." He risked a glance at Adeline.

Her expression didn't change; she was listening just as intently as his brothers were. Because they didn't know the story either. He felt weird talking about his past but he wanted the sheriff to have the whole picture.

"He found out and got pissed. We got in a stupid fistfight. No weapons or anything, just two barely eighteen-year-olds being dumbasses. And that was it between us. The girl..." Hell, Mac couldn't even remember her name. It started with an S or something. "She moved away for college and I don't think she ever moved back. Not long after our fight, Harlan ended up getting sent away for robbery. Or something, I don't even know the details. I heard he got out, then got tossed right back in for another robbery. This one escalated or something. Which you probably already know?"

Lincoln simply nodded.

"I joined the Marines not long after and put that guy in my rearview. But then I just found out there might be a meth lab on his property. It's far enough away from our house but it still borders our property. And I heard it just blew up." He'd already told Lincoln some of this but he wanted Adeline to know too. Because she wasn't going anywhere while she was still in danger. "So I think with his meth lab blowing up so close to where I live, and our contentious past... I'm an easy target. Just guessing though." He wasn't going to admit to blowing up the meth house. Nope. But he hoped Lincoln understood what he was saying.

Lincoln lifted an eyebrow. "There was a fire. A gas explosion, I heard. It's not in my territory though. The Harrison PD is saying it was an accident."

"What does the fire department say?"

"That it looks like there might have been drug production there at one time. Everything's destroyed, however. They also found the remnants of what they suspect is a grenade." He gave Mac a hard look.

Mac lifted a shoulder.

Luckily Lincoln didn't ask any more questions. Not like Mac would tell the truth anyway, but still.

"If he thinks you had anything to do with hurting his income, it explains why he came after you. Even if you didn't have a history together. But that's just going to add fuel to the fire." Lincoln continued. "I'm currently getting an arrest warrant for him. I need official statements from both of you as well. I need details of everything that happened at your shop." He looked between Adeline and Mac. "Is that a problem?"

Adeline shook her head. "No, I'll make a statement. That lunatic came after us with a gun."

"On the phone you said he wasn't alone." Lincoln looked back at Mac. "Did you get a good look at any of the people he was with?"

"No, but we might be able to get something on one of my security cameras. I just need to pull the feeds up. Do you...know how badly my shop was damaged?"

"It doesn't look great," Lincoln said quietly. "I'm sorry. It's not completely destroyed but the east side of the building is basically demolished. Easton is there with the rest of the fire crew," he said, referring to his brother and one of Mac's friends. "He's taking pictures for you for insurance. I let him know you might not be able to get down there right away so he's got you covered."

Mac wasn't surprised; he and Easton went way back and were fairly tight. "I'll get in contact with him later. Thank you for meeting us here."

"Sure. I'm going to keep deputies at both your places, and while I can't tell you what to do, I think it'll be smart if you all stay here. I don't think any of you should go home. The law enforcement presence is likely going to keep Harlan and any of his guys away, but the windows of your rental car were smashed in and the tires were all slashed," he said to Adeline. "He might know who you are."

She wrapped her arms around herself, and as if they choreographed it, both his brothers slid an arm around her. Her curls were down tonight, and in her Christmas sweater and jeans she looked so...young, and exhausted. And he hated that she was in this situation because of him.

He wished he was holding her, wished he hadn't screwed things up between them, and that he had the right to comfort her.

"If it's okay with these guys, I'll stay here," Adeline said. "If not, I can—"

"Of course you're staying!" Joe said before Mac could utter a word.

"Yeah," Dylan said even as Mac nodded.

"Of course you're going to stay. I'm not letting you leave," Mac said.

She lifted an eyebrow at him but didn't otherwise respond.

"What do you guys need? Food? Bedding? I can ask my mom to get some meals together and you know she'll be more than happy to." Lincoln's expression softened when he looked at Adeline. "She'll bring you one of her specialty pies if you ask."

"I want to tell you not to go to any trouble but I love your mom's cooking," she said with a sheepish grin. "Do you guys have any food here?" She looked at the three of them.

"No. We have a case of bottled water and probably some sports drinks," Mac said dryly. And it was only left over from when they'd been working on the place.

"I'll take care of it." Lincoln looked at his cell phone when it buzzed. He quickly tucked it away. "For now, sit tight. We've got an arrest warrant issued for Harlan and we're going to find him. Try not to show your faces in the front yard or anything. It shouldn't take long to track down Harlan. But with his father being chief of police in Harrison, I'm playing this carefully. Don't go anywhere if you can avoid it."

Mac nodded and pushed away from the window as his brothers and Adeline stood.

"I'll do a food drop off-later this evening. I'm going to call my mom as soon as I leave. I know she's got frozen meals stocked up so I might just bring a couple over tonight and then we'll get you some staples and basics so you're covered the next couple days."

"Thank you," Adeline said, her voice thick, and Mac realized she was close to tears.

Of course she was. *Hell.* They'd just been shot at, gone on the run from a lunatic, and now she was stuck here with him.

The sheriff gave her a hug. "Of course nothing will happen to you, I promise. Autumn and Serenity would have my head." His voice was slightly lighter, as if he was trying to ease the tension.

She sniffled and wiped away a couple tears that started to fall.

As soon as Mac shut the door behind Lincoln, he pulled her into a hug. Because screw it. Adeline crying was too much.

She was stiff in his arms for a moment but then hugged him back, burying her face against his chest as her body shook slightly.

He squeezed her tighter, protectiveness roaring through him. "It's going to be okay. No one is going to get to any of us." He would do anything to protect her and his brothers—or die trying.

CHAPTER SEVENTEEN

"Thank you again for cooking dinner." Adeline looked over at Dylan, who'd made some sort of chicken, cheese and broccoli casserole. Lincoln's mother had covertly ended up dropping off some supplies, food-stuffs, and frozen casseroles. Instead of cooking one of those, Dylan had opted to make something else for all of them.

Right now she was focusing on food and anything *not* what had happened to them a couple hours ago. She was having a hell of a time processing being shot at, the sudden violence of it all. It brought up ugly memories, ones she liked to keep locked up.

"Thanks," he murmured, his cheeks actually flushing. Which was sort of adorable. He was twenty or maybe twenty-one and huge, but he was sweet, and she was pretty sure shy as well.

"Mac taught both of us to cook. Said it was important. You know, for the ladies," Joe tacked on. Because of course he did. He was so unaffected by everything, didn't even seem to mind that they were all stuck here and couldn't go home.

Mac practically choked and shook his head, his expression unreadable as he looked at Adeline. "I never said they needed to learn to cook for the ladies," he muttered.

"Pretty sure you did," Dylan said, grinning, shrugging off some of his quietness. "You said, and I think this is a quote, that 'no woman will keep a man around if he can't take care of himself.'"

"That's pretty good advice." Adeline grinned. Being with them eased some of the tension coiled tight inside her. "And your brother's not wrong," she said to Dylan. "You nailed it with this meal, by the way. You should definitely make it for your future woman."

Not responding, he stood and took her empty plate as well as his, still blushing.

"You're going to blow up his ego," Mac muttered, looking kind of surly now as he leaned back in his chair. In jeans and a flannel shirt with the sleeves shoved up to his elbows, he was rocking that lumberjack vibe. God, he was delicious.

"You don't believe in complimenting the chef?"

"I didn't say that."

"No, he just likes to keep us humble." Joe stood and grabbed his own plate. "You guys want to play any games or watch TV?" he asked as he headed to the sink and dropped his plate in it. "Who knows how long we'll be stuck here."

A shiver rolled through her. She hated not knowing anything, that they had to be dependent on what the deputies did until they could go home.

"I don't know if you guys want to play with Adeline," Mac murmured.

His brothers looked at him in horror.

"He's not insulting me," she said. "He just knows that I am a *superior* game player and he wants to spare you from being destroyed by my awesomeness."

She grinned at the shock on the brothers' faces. This was so much better than obsessing over the fact that some guy wanted to kill Mac, and apparently her.

She stood, pushing the chair back, and started clearing off the silverware and napkins. "It's true, I'm an absolute savage and I will destroy both of you. My motto is if you're not first, you're last." Her mother had always told her that her competitiveness would get her into trouble too, but she didn't care. She liked to win.

Mac snickered, the rumble coming from his chest way too damn sexy as both Dylan and Joe started to laugh.

"How about we meet back in the living room in twenty minutes?" Joe asked. "I'm going to call Marcy really quick."

"Works for me. And I'll clean up, since you cooked." She nudged Dylan away from the sink.

But Mac quickly took over and in turn shooed her away. "I've got this. You don't need to clean anything up. It's my fault you're in this mess, so go relax."

She certainly wasn't going to argue with anyone to wash dishes, and they hadn't had their dishwasher installed yet. "It's not anyone's fault but that Harlan Hayward. But thanks. Where are the board games? Crap, do you *have* any? The place is pretty new."

"There's a stack of boxes on the bookshelf in the living room. We added them as extras for potential renters. Some of them aren't even opened."

"I get to pick the game, then," she said.

"I'm kind of glad that my brothers get to see you like this."

She simply grinned at him and left the kitchen. Things had shifted between them again. Or maybe it was just wishful thinking on her part. She suspected now why he'd blown her off at least.

But now that all that was a moot point, what did that mean for them? She was feeling way too raw and vulnerable to think about asking him.

Some lunatic wanted her dead simply because he thought she was Mac's woman—and sadly she wasn't. She'd cried her eyes out on Mac's shirt earlier. And now things were in a sort of weird holding pattern, and right around Christmas at that.

Yeah, she was so *not* putting herself out there with Mac again. She just wanted to get through this unscathed.

* * *

"Boom!" Adeline took Mac's last Monopoly dollar after he paid her for landing on Boardwalk. She put the money in the pile she had deemed her "Mac pile of money" and threw her hands up in the air like she'd just finished a marathon. She knew she was acting a little overboard right now, but it was the only thing keeping her from going crazy with worry. "That's how it's done, son!"

Joe and Dylan cackled with laughter. "I'm just glad we don't have to see Mac's stupid victory dance," Dylan said.

She'd noticed that Dylan was starting to come out of his shell more. Or maybe he was always like this, but just around his brothers. Either way, she liked it.

"Stupid? My dance is amazing." Even though Mac had a surly expression in place, his mouth curved up slightly as if he was fighting a smile. Every so often he got up and did a quick scan of the windows and backyard, a reminder that they had to be vigilant—not that she needed one, no matter how silly she was acting.

"Well I wouldn't know, since I've never seen you win." She gave Mac a pointed look.

He gave her a real smile then and oh boy, she felt it all the way to her toes. "The day is coming, you'll see."

"Promises, promises."

"You are *always* invited to game night now," Joe said.

"No way! The three of you ganged up on me." Mac started organizing all the money, putting it into neat stacks.

"You deserve it after years of destroying us." Dylan's tone was dry.

"She's not even a good winner. She's lording it over us."

"Says the man who has a *victory* dance." Adeline shook her head. "Sore, sore loser, Mac."

"Really?" Mac nodded to her T-shirt which she'd changed into.

It said *If you're not first, you're last* across the front. It had been in her bag of clothes that Lincoln had dropped off—and she had no doubt that Serenity or Autumn had included this for her. She was glad to have it—it was one of her favorite T-shirts to wear to quilting class and gave her a sense of normalcy. "Fair enough."

"I'm probably going to go FaceTime with Marcy for a while," Joe said, stifling a yawn.

"Yeah, I'll probably crash too." Dylan stood and stretched. "Unless you want me to stay up and keep an eye on things?" He looked to Mac for guidance, the respect for his older brother undeniable.

"No, go get some sleep. I'm going to take first shift. You can take over in the morning. We'll work in shifts."

"You want me to keep you company?" Adeline helped him to clean up the board and little pieces. His brothers had scattered everything around, not exactly helping, and it made her smile.

"Yeah, that'd be great. I think Lincoln said there was some hot chocolate in one of the bags his mom dropped off."

"Hot chocolate *and* marshmallows. I peeked already. You want some?"

"Yeah, thanks."

The look he gave her in that moment was... Well, she wasn't exactly sure how to read it. And she was too wound up to worry about that right now.

Combined with everything else, it caused way too much tension low in her belly.

She simply wanted him too much. Every second she was around him and his brothers, she got to see this sweet, real side to him. When she'd first met him, she'd thought he was this sort of stoic loner, but no, he was simply a good big brother. And the sexiest man she'd ever met.

But none of that mattered now. Nothing did until they got their lives back.

CHAPTER EIGHTEEN

*A*deline screamed, pressing on her mother's chest, trying to stop the flow of blood but it just kept coming. There was so much, covering her fingers as she tried to will it back inside her.

"No!" She screamed it again as she tore off her shirt, balled it up to hold it against the multiple wounds. No, no, no. "Please don't die," she begged. "You can't die."

Pain exploded in her side and suddenly she was flying through the air. He'd kicked her.

Then he was standing over her, his dark eyes wild with rage, endless pits of evil as he stared down at her. He held a gun in his hand. "You're next," he snarled.

A siren sounded in the distance and he turned, distracted.

A wild survival instinct took over and she kicked out, slamming her foot against his knee. Screaming, he fell, his arms flailing back at the sudden kick. He slipped in the pool of blood, his gun flying out of his hands.

She jumped to her feet and ran out the still open front door. And she kept running, waiting for the bullet in her back that never came.

Her eyes snapped open with a jerk, her breath raspy, uneven. It had just been a dream—a nightmare.

A low rumbling filled the air. That must be what had startled Adeline out of her shallow sleep. She shoved up from the bed, taking in the unfamiliar room in seconds. Sheer floor-to-ceiling white curtains covered a big window with bamboo blinds firmly in place. Pale gray walls, no art on them, and a queen-sized bed with a fluffy gray and teal comforter. Two sleek, feminine lamps with crystal bases were on the nightstands. She was in a sparsely furnished room of Mac's rental house.

Not back in...that place. She hadn't been there in a very long time. It was just taking her brain a moment to catch up with reality.

She jerked again at another rumbling sound as she glanced at the clock on the nightstand. Four in the morning. What was that... It sounded like a motorcycle gang was rolling down the street.

What if it was Harlan coming to finish the job? Panicked, she shoved the tangled comforter out of the way and hurried into the hall to find both Joe and Dylan stepping out of the other bedroom. They all hurried to the living room where Mac stood by the window.

Joe was faster than all of them and rushed to the other front-facing window, peeking past the curtains.

At his snicker, the tension in her shoulders eased.

And that was when she noticed that Mac had a grin on his face too. He was clearly not concerned, so at least she knew they weren't being attacked by the gun-wielding lunatic from yesterday.

She moved in close to Mac, ignoring his masculine, earthy scent as she peered out the window.

She blinked to see a woman and a man on a motorcycle... Going at it. Like actually having sex on the motorcycle while it was running. "What the hell is wrong with those people?" she muttered. Sleep still lingered at the edge of her senses.

"Who cares? It's a great show," Dylan murmured.

She looked at him in shock, and even in the dimness, she saw his cheeks flush.

"I m-mean..." he stuttered.

"We know what you mean," Mac murmured, giving him a light shove on the shoulder. "Apparently these guys get off on being watched."

"Yeah, well, at four in the morning they're jerks." Adeline stepped back from the window. She noticed that all three brothers stayed to watch. "And you guys are perverts." It was out before she could stop herself. She was going to blame it on lack of sleep—she'd tossed and turned all night, worried Hayward would find them.

They turned to look at her as one unit and they all shrugged, which was for some reason ridiculously adorable.

But Mac peeled himself away from the window while the others continued to watch and give commentary.

"If he's not careful, he's gonna burn his leg on the tailpipe." Dylan shook his head slightly, as if he was narrating a football game or something.

"I bet it's worth it," Joe added.

"Why don't you head back to bed? Get a few more hours of sleep," Mac said to her.

"Me? Have you gotten any rest?"

He lifted a shoulder.

"Why don't you snag a couple hours in my bed?" She realized how that sounded and felt her cheeks flame. "Ah,

I mean, alone. Go grab some shut-eye for a while? I'm sure you need it."

Heat flared in his gaze but he shook his head slightly. "Nah, I'll just sneak like an hour in a bit. A power nap. I'm good. I'll cook us all breakfast first. Dylan isn't the only one who knows how to cook in this family." She couldn't quite read his tone.

She frowned at his retreating back and followed him into the kitchen. "Did you teach your brothers to cook?"

"More or less," he said as he opened the fridge and started pulling stuff out.

Lincoln and whoever he had enlisted to load them up with foodstuffs had gone overboard, and it was highly appreciated. Adeline's money was on her friends and Lincoln's mom for the abundance of things.

Adeline had received multiple texts from both Serenity and Autumn telling her that if she needed something to simply ask. And Adeline had texted Bianca to let her know what was going on in the briefest way possible. Her friend was worried but had also offered to help out. Adeline didn't want any of them involved in this, however. She wanted them far, far away from this tangled mess.

She started making coffee, inhaling the rich scent as it started percolating, already waking up from the smell alone. Now that she was out of bed, she wouldn't be able to go back to sleep anyway. She was one of those people that once she was up, she was up for the rest of the day.

"I'm thinking either omelets or scrambled eggs. Or I can whip up some pancakes."

Surprised, she turned from the coffee maker, leaning against the countertop as she eyed Mac.

The man was sexy as hell, his T-shirt stretching across his broad shoulders, down to his tapered waist. He was this beautiful work of art that she wanted to paint—and run her fingers all over. "Do you mean from scratch?"

"We've got one of those shake-and-pour pancake batter mixes. But for the record, I *can* make pancakes from scratch."

"Eggs actually sounds better. I'll take them however you cook them."

"Well, what's your preference? Because my brothers are animals and don't care."

She snickered slightly, able to hear them still offering commentary from the other room on the exploits of the couple outside. Men really were ridiculous sometimes. "Omelets are my preference. I think we've got peppers, mushrooms, cheese too. I want it all."

"Omelets it is. How does southwest sound?"

Her stomach rumbled in response and she grinned. "That sounds like perfection."

"So did you get any sleep last night?" he asked as he opened the egg carton.

"A little bit. More than you, that's for sure. But I tossed and turned. I guess my brain just wouldn't shut off." And the trauma of everything had brought up bad memories, even though the two things weren't related. But knowing someone wanted them dead must have triggered something in her brain. She'd felt so safe for so long, and now...it was hard to go back to that constant fight-or-flight state her mind seemed to be in. Someone had shot at them yesterday, and that monster had made it clear he'd do more than just shoot her. She knew that no place was truly safe, but still, it had been so casually violent.

"You've been through a lot."

"We both have, not just me."

"Sadly, that wasn't the first time I was shot at."

"That doesn't make me feel better," she said as the coffee maker rumbled behind her. "Does that mean you weren't terrified?" He'd been so damn calm and in control yesterday and she'd felt as if she could come apart at the seams.

"That's hard to answer. For the record, I do *not* like being shot at. And yes, it's a scary thing, but...my brain sort of shut off and my training kicked into gear. My only goal when he was shooting at us was to get you to safety and get us out of range. I guess my brain just broke things down into achievable goals. It's the only way I can think to describe it."

She had a whole new level of respect for him. "Meanwhile, my brain was screaming that we were going to get blown away and all I could think about was how painful it would be to get shot."

He turned back to the stove and started cracking eggs. Then he paused and looked at her, his expression almost horrified, as if he'd just realized something. "This must have brought up bad memories for you."

She started to shake her head but then nodded. "A little, yeah." She didn't want to load guilt onto him though. It wasn't like he'd wanted this to happen.

"I'm sorry, Adeline. And I'm sorry I dragged you into this."

"You didn't do anything. I just happened to be in the wrong place at the wrong time." She inwardly winced. Because she'd gone to his workshop to basically yell at him. She cleared her throat. "About the reason I came to see you..." Why was she opening this can of worms? Because she wanted to talk about it and get this over with so there would be no lingering awkwardness.

"The reason I blew you off is because I thought something like this might happen with Harlan." His tone was neutral enough, but she heard underlying emotion there. Anger maybe. Not at her though, but himself.

She'd figured that out, but wanted it all spelled out for her own peace of mind. "So you didn't text me telling me that you'd changed your mind because you...realized you weren't really attracted to me?" The looks he'd given her told her he was still into her, but yep, she was feeling all sorts of raw and needed clarification.

He turned around and looked at her as if she was crazy. "I thought things might escalate with Harlan. So I was taking precautions because the last thing I ever want is for you to be in danger. But here we are." Disgust laced his words. Self-disgust, she realized.

"It's not your fault."

"Sure feels that way." He turned around and she got the feeling the conversation was over. For now anyway.

But she wasn't letting this go completely.

* * *

"Someone's phone is ringing," Joe said as he stepped into the kitchen.

It took Adeline a second to realize that it was hers, coming from the bedroom. They'd just finished breakfast and she was working on her third cup of coffee right now. She hurried to grab it, and answered Lincoln's call on her way back to the kitchen. "Yeah?"

"Hey, hope I didn't wake you."

"No, we've been up." She mouthed the word sheriff to the three men in the kitchen as she headed straight for her coffee.

"Someone tried to break into your house about three hours ago. I would've called you sooner but I didn't see the point in waking you up since we don't need a statement or anything. We got the guy in custody and he has ties to Harlan."

Someone had been at her house? Ice slicked up her spine. "I'm going to put you on speaker," she said so the others could hear and she didn't have to repeat everything. As she did, she quickly said, "Someone with ties to Harlan broke into my house." So the guy obviously knew who she was. The realization settled hard in her stomach.

"He attempted to," Lincoln said over the line. "He's on something, so we've got him in a cell while he sleeps it off. He hasn't asked for a lawyer, so I'm hoping once he rouses we'll be able to question him while he's sober."

"What's his name?"

After Lincoln answered, Mac shrugged. "I don't know him."

"You wouldn't. He lives two towns over and has a very long rap sheet. I just wanted to let you guys know. I hate to say it but you've all still got to sit tight. Don't do anything about this," Lincoln added. "Mac, I am specifically talking to you."

He held up his hands in a defensive motion as if the sheriff could see him. "I'm not going to do anything. I wouldn't leave my brothers or Adeline. We're all staying here."

"Good. Just keep your phones on you and let me know if you see anything out of the ordinary."

"We will," she said. After they ended the call, she set her phone on the countertop. "Mac, we took a vote and you're going to go get a couple hours of sleep."

He blinked in clear surprise, looking between the three of them. "You all voted?"

"Yep. When you stepped out to make a phone call earlier we all voted on it, and it's three against one. So deal with it."

"You guys are being ridiculous."

"No, what would be ridiculous was if you argued with us," Dylan said. He was definitely out of his shell now. And Adeline was glad he was comfortable to be himself around her. "If you want to be on top of your game, you need more than a sad hour of sleep. We're all here and it's fairly early morning. We can all keep an eye on things while you doze."

Mac crossed those sexy arms over his chest. "You're all ganging up on me now?"

Adeline put her hands on her hips. "If that's what it takes, yes." Then she stepped forward and grasped his shoulders, manhandling him and physically turning him toward the hallway. She knew that if he didn't want to move, there was no way she could actually make him.

But with a sigh he headed toward the bedroom with her. She heard his brothers laughing lightly behind them and ignored them. "You need to set a good example for them anyway. You can't be a stubborn jackass and refuse to sleep for no reason."

"You're very bossy." His deep voice was a balm to her frayed nerves.

"That's correct. I'm a bossy queen of board games. Now you know more about me," she said as she nudged him into the bedroom.

She'd made up the bed a little while ago and her meager belongings were still in her duffel next to it. "I've got the white noise machine going and we will definitely keep it down." He opened his mouth to say something but she shook her head. "There is literally no reason for you to argue with us. Rest, you'll feel better. If you don't, I'm going to ask you questions about blowing up that meth house. Because even though you didn't admit to it, I'm pretty sure you were behind it. It's why Hayward is so pissed at you, right?"

He simply gritted his teeth. "Fine. I'll get a little bit of sleep."

Ha, that was answer enough. "Thank you." Adeline shut the door behind her and met his brothers in the kitchen.

"I can't believe he listened to us," Joe murmured as he dried a plate.

"He didn't listen to us," Dylan said. "He listened to *her*. And we are definitely keeping you around," he added.

Warmth spread through her at his words. She didn't want to get used to hanging out with them, but being around them made her miss her mom, made her feel like she could be part of their family. Which was so ridiculous she couldn't even believe herself. "Did you bring your laptop?" she asked Joe.

"Yes. Are you ready to get to work?"

She glanced over her shoulder, knowing Mac wouldn't like what they were about to do, but that was just too bad. When they'd voted on ordering Mac to sleep they'd also talked about a couple other things. Now that someone had been at her house, tried to break in, she was even more determined to take things into her own hands. "Let's do this."

CHAPTER NINETEEN

"What are you guys doing?" Mac asked as he stared at his brothers and Adeline. The three of them were sitting around the coffee table while Adeline typed quickly on Joe's computer. Her expression was intense.

She froze, and they all looked up at him, guilt flickering in each of their eyes. *Uh-oh.*

He hadn't meant to sleep so long but he'd crashed hard, surrounded by the scent of Adeline on the sheets and comforter. It was now late afternoon but he *did* feel a lot better. He still had shit to do—like figure out what he could salvage at his shop and deal with his insurance company on top of everything else, but... "What are you guys doing?" he repeated.

"We've been looking into Harlan." Adeline leaned back, jutting her chin out defiantly. "We've found out that he's got a girlfriend, though they seem to fight a lot, given some of her social media posts."

He scrubbed a hand over his face and sat on the couch across from them. "How can you know all this?"

"Because his girlfriend does a lot of stuff publicly. Especially when she's mad at him," Dylan said.

"She likes posting bikini pictures," Joe added.

"So I created a fake profile of a hot guy and be-friended her on Instagram," Adeline added. "We're going to see if we can get anything on Harlan through her."

"She's not going to fall for that," he said, shaking his head, both annoyed and impressed. "And you guys need to leave this alone. Lincoln is handling it."

"She already invited Adeline's fake Insta profile to a party tonight." Joe's look was far too smug.

"We've been exchanging messages," she said, laughing lightly. "She's *really* not faithful to her boyfriend. I told her I'm new to the area, that I just moved from Miami. She really likes Miami and we've been talking about places to go. She might have been testing me to see if I really knew about the area. I must have passed her test because she invited 'me' to this thing tonight."

Trying to wake up more, he looked between the three of them, unable to believe that this was what they'd been doing the last few hours. Lincoln had specifically asked them to keep a low profile. "Guys, the sheriff is handling this."

"This guy tried to shoot us—to kill us," Adeline said. "He burned down your shop. I'm not taking this lying down. I start back to work next week and I'm not going to live in fear. We're not actually going to the party as ourselves, but we can drive by, see if we can find something out and let the sheriff know if we see Harlan. That's it. We just want to find him. The sooner he's in jail, the sooner we can all go back to our lives."

Mac suppressed a sigh. "Guys, I need to talk to Adeline alone."

He was glad when his brothers actually got up and hurried from the room.

She stood too, doing that hands-on-hips thing that was waaaaay too sexy. She looked like a hot librarian who wanted to order him around. Her curls bounced as she stepped forward. "I'm not going to sit here and do nothing," she said before he could even say a word.

"Fine," he muttered.

"Wait...what?" Some of her attitude disappeared.

"Well, I *know* you're not going to listen to reason, that you're just going to do whatever you want. And short of tying you up and keeping you here, I can't force you to stay." Her eyes flared with something that looked a lot like heat at the tying thing, but he kept talking, tucking that intriguing nugget away for later. "So, we will act as a *team*. One where I'm in charge. I'll give this information to Lincoln. If for some reason he doesn't do anything with it—which he will, so this is a moot point—we will simply drive by wherever this party is. That's it," he said.

She narrowed her eyes at him. "You're being very amenable."

He lifted a shoulder. He wasn't really, but was glad she thought so. He understood needing to do something, to not be stuck on the sidelines and let someone else be in charge. Right now he hated that the four of them were cooped up inside what was essentially a safe house. But his main concern was protecting his brothers and Adeline.

Even from themselves.

Because he knew Lincoln would take this information and use it.

"I'm hungry," he murmured, his gaze falling to her mouth as he thought about eating a lot more than food. God, he wanted to devour her. But that wasn't going to happen. He'd gotten her into this shit situation, no way would she want anything to do with him again. "Have you guys eaten yet?"

She watched him for a long moment, then shook her head. "Let's go grab something."

CHAPTER TWENTY

In the interrogation room, Lincoln sat across the table from Ian Shaw—the man who'd attempted to break into Adeline's house yesterday. Or technically early this morning. The guy had sobered up, though he was still sporting bloodshot eyes and was staring at Lincoln mutinously.

"Here's the soda you requested," he said as he slid the can across the table. He tried to keep the annoyance out of his voice. Lincoln needed this guy to talk.

Wordlessly Ian took it, popped the top with a snap and chugged it in seconds. Then he sighed and let his head roll back, his Adam's apple bobbing up and down as he slumped against the chair.

"Why were you breaking into Adeline Rodriguez's house?" Lincoln asked.

"Don't I get a lawyer?"

"I have offered you a lawyer three times and you have declined." But if he was asking now, Lincoln would make the call. He pushed his chair back and stood. "Are you officially asking for an attorney?"

"Maybe."

"There is no maybe. You either are or you aren't. I'm not playing games, Ian." He had things to do—leads to follow up on. They were short-staffed. And with an arrest warrant out on Harlan Hayward, everyone was working round the clock trying to find the guy. And that was on top of handling normal calls for the entire county.

"The last court-appointed attorney I had was a moron," Ian grumbled as he traced his finger up and down the side of the green can. "If I tell you what I know, I want all charges dropped."

Lincoln frowned at him. The balls on this asshole. "Why would I do that?"

"If I tell you about a murder and some planned murders, I want the charges dropped for this stupid B and E."

"Murder?" That definitely changed things. Lincoln had wanted details on Harlan's whereabouts and the fire at Mac's shop. But murder...

"Yeah. Committed by Harlan Hayward." Ian leaned back in his chair, his expression smug as he crossed one leg over the other.

"If you're serious, I'll get the district attorney in here to draw up the paperwork. They're not going to charge you with breaking and entering if you have real information. But you'll have to offer up something real."

"The information *is* real. And I know where the body is."

Lincoln's heart rate kicked up, but he kept his expression neutral. "You better not be screwing with me."

"I'm not. He's lost his mind." Ian leaned forward, the chair scraping against the floor, and instead of smugness a trickle of fear bled into his dark eyes. "He's *angry*. Angry at everyone, it seems. But especially that Mac Collins guy. Says he blew up his trailer. Says the guy is an asshole who he should have taken out a long time ago."

Lincoln decided that Ian knew exactly what he was talking about. He couldn't prove that Mac had blown up Harlan's trailer but his instinct told him that Mac had. It was likely why he'd been targeted by Harlan. And the fact that they already had bad blood over a woman only fanned the flames. "Why'd you break into Adeline's house?"

"I want a deal first."

Lincoln shoved up from his chair. He had to get the district attorney for this. "I'll be back soon."

Ian lifted his chained hands and shook them slightly. "I'm not going anywhere."

* * *

"Is the paperwork to your satisfaction?" Jada Sanchez—the district attorney—asked Ian, who'd read over the agreement five times.

Lincoln sat next to her quietly on their side of the table as Ian kept reading. Ian really should just get a lawyer, but the guy *really* hated them. Said he was done with their incompetence and them screwing him over.

Either way, if his information was good, no charges would be brought. Lincoln didn't love making deals like this, but Ian was a petty thief and Lincoln had no doubt he'd end up in jail again. Here or elsewhere. Some people simply couldn't stay on the right path, and unfortunately

Ian didn't even appear to try. Setting him free in exchange for information about a murder was serving the greater good.

"It looks fine." Ian finally signed his name and slid it across to Jada, who then signed in turn. She nodded at Lincoln, the corner of her mouth curving up ever so slightly. She was smart, could smell a big bust in the water.

Normally Jada would take over at this point but she'd already told Lincoln to do the talking, that she had a feeling this guy would respond better to a man.

So he turned back to Ian who was basically ignoring Jada, except to glance at her breasts every now and then. *What a piece of work.*

Lincoln forced his expression to remain neutral, however. If there had really been a murder and if Harlan was planning another one—other than Mac—he had to keep his cool. "You said you had information. Talk or this is void." He tapped the piece of paper once.

"The other night Mac Collins blew up Harlan's trailer. Or he thinks Collins did," Ian said. "I don't have proof or anything and I'm not accusing him," he said, looking between the two of them. "But that's what set Harlan off. I've never seen him like that." Some of his swagger faded as he straightened slightly in his chair. "He got pissed and just...stabbed Brandon." He shivered slightly. "It was over so fast."

"Who is Brandon?" Jada asked. "We need a full name."

"Brandon Jenkins."

Lincoln knew that name. Jenkins was known for making meth and had been arrested five times that Lincoln could remember. "Where did this happen?"

"On his father's property. Where he was running that meth lab. Brandon…was making the shit for him. I showed up with my boy Big D to take Brandon out for beers and to a strip club. He's always up for a good time. But we came back early and…boom." He made an explosion motion with his hands. "It was sick. Brandon called Harlan about it and within minutes of showing up—" He made a stabbing motion with his hands.

"You're saying for the record that you saw Harlan Hayward stab Brandon Jenkins?" Jada asked.

"Yeah, lady! I saw it. He gutted him, just stabbed right into his gut, then cut upward. It was…" He swallowed hard. "There was no need to kill him. It wasn't his fault."

Lincoln made a mental note to ask who "Big D" was, but had a feeling he already knew.

Ian continued. "Someone, an anonymous someone I guess, made a call to the cops about the explosion. That's what really set Harlan off. He went on a rampage. I thought he'd kill me if I didn't go along with what he wanted."

"Why is he convinced that Mac Collins blew up his place?" Lincoln asked.

"No idea. He doesn't tell me everything."

"What's the nature of your relationship with Harlan?" Jada asked, the tone of her voice calm and neutral.

Ian cleared his throat. "We party together. Have a good time, that's all. Mainly I was friends with Brandon, which is how I got tangled up with Harlan."

Yeah right. Ian worked for Harlan, likely sold his product, but that wasn't Lincoln's concern right now. "Were you with Harlan when he went by Collins's shop?"

He paused, then nodded. "I didn't help him set the place on fire. Am I going to be charged for any of this?" He looked at Jada now, actually at her face, trying to show some respect.

"No. If you're telling the truth, then we will not be pressing charges against you. But if you're lying, this entire agreement is void."

He shoved out a breath. "I stayed in the car and suddenly he ran out after shooting up the place. I told him to stop—and so did Big D. He told me to shut the fuck up. Then he punched me in the face and pulled his gun on Big D. From there, he set the place on fire and slashed the tires of the car in the parking lot. He was like a rabid animal, man."

"How did he know who Adeline Rodriguez was? Had he seen her before?"

"Nah. He got a bunch of paperwork from the car. Got her name and address."

"Why'd he want you to break into her place?" Lincoln knew the answer but wanted to hear him say it.

Ian cleared his throat again. "He wanted me to break into the Rodriguez woman's place to see if she was there and then kidnap her. But I'm no kidnapper! I just waited until I was sure she wasn't home before breaking in."

"How could you tell she wasn't home?"

"I kept an eye on the place for about twelve hours on and off, and there was no movement. No lights or anything. And her mail was still in her mailbox. I was simply going to break in, steal some shit and then tell him she wasn't home—which was the truth." He lifted a shoulder, but Lincoln could see the fear in his eyes. "I knew if I did nothing, he'd kill me too. I figured this would buy me some time."

"What did he do with Brandon Jenkins's body?" Jada asked, drawing the conversation back to the murder.

"There's a pond on his dad's property—or his property now, I guess. I think his dad sold it or gave it to him or—"

"Ian." Lincoln needed the guy to stay focused.

"Right. There's a pond about two miles from where his trailer is. He tied bricks to it and dumped it. I can't know for sure, but I don't think it's the first body he's tossed there." Sweat popped out along Ian's forehead. "He did it far too easily. Like…he'd had practice."

"Is his father involved with his meth production?" Jada asked. She was going in for the kill now.

But Ian shook his head. "No way. Don't get me wrong, I think his dad is an asshole. But he wouldn't be involved with drugs. He told Harlan that he needed to get his life together and get a real job," he said in a mocking voice. "If he'd known that Harlan was running meth, he probably would've killed him."

Lincoln didn't like any of this, but his mind was already turning. They had enough to get a warrant to search the pond and the property. This was turning into a real shit show. "Where is Harlan now?"

"I dunno. Well, I know he's gone after Collins and the woman. And Collins's brothers, even though they have nothing to do with this. He's pretty pissed at his own girlfriend right now too. He's got a whole freaking list of people he's angry at." Ian rubbed a hand over his face. "I'm sure I'm on it now too for not coming through."

"Does he seriously have a hit list?"

"Yeah. After what he did at Collins's shop, he said it was only a matter of time before the sheriff's department got a warrant on him. I think he's going for broke. I think he's going to kill as many people as possible out of revenge. I could be wrong but... He was talking pretty wild, saying some crazy shit. It's the only reason I agreed to break into the Rodriguez woman's house. I didn't want him to gut me right then and there."

Lincoln nodded and stood. They were off to a good start and he wanted to keep Ian talking. "Want me to grab you a Sprite? Or food?"

"Yeah, I could go for an Italian hoagie. And some chips. Doritos. And a macadamia nut cookie."

"I'll get it. While I'm gone, you keep talking. You tell DA Sanchez everything you know."

The man nodded and straightened in his chair slightly. Ready to do whatever it took to save his own skin.

CHAPTER TWENTY-ONE

Mac eyed Harlan's girlfriend through his binoculars. Mac had finally given in to Adeline and his brothers. But only because Lincoln hadn't returned *any* of his calls. They'd borrowed an SUV from a friend and now Joe and Dylan were in the back and Adeline and Mac were in the front. They were tucked away in a neighboring parking lot next to the restaurant Harlan's girlfriend had mentioned to Adeline's alter ego on Instagram. A dumpster and oak tree hid them well.

"Let me look through the binoculars." Adeline held out her hand as she squinted through the windshield across the darkened parking lots.

He'd let her drive because he wanted his hands free, but he wasn't happy to be here. Mac knew they were in minimal danger right now. Probably the same level as if they'd been at the rental house. Still, he knew they shouldn't have left. But guilt at dragging Adeline into all this inadvertently had eaten away at his resolve.

The sheriff's department had a warrant out for Harlan's arrest, and he knew they'd find him. Eventually. But Mac also knew the department only had so many people working for them and they had limited resources. Adeline had argued that they'd already managed to track down Harlan's girlfriend to what had turned out not to be exactly a party, but a bar with an outdoor party going on.

He handed his binoculars to her and she moved them slightly until she saw who they'd been looking for. Harlan Hayward's girlfriend—Karen Carter—with a bunch of her girlfriends. No Harlan though.

Not that Mac had actually expected him to show up, but the others had been insistent they not stay home and "do nothing." Unfortunately Mac understood that sometimes "doing nothing" actually meant you just had to be patient. But he'd gotten Adeline into this situation, and pure guilt was what had gotten him to agree to this asinine driving expedition. Hell, maybe they'd see something useful.

"We're being careful," Joe said from the back, though Mac hadn't said anything. But his tension and annoyance at all of them was likely palpable, like a beating drum invading the quiet of the SUV.

So here they were, two towns over in the parking lot across from a seafood restaurant and bar that overlooked a brightly lit lake. Lights were strung up over the back patio but most of the furniture had seen better days, from what he'd spotted through the binoculars. About forty people were out on the back patio, all loud, their voices carrying over the two parking lots. And likely all drunk.

Adeline stiffened. Suddenly she shoved the binoculars at Mac. "Is that him?"

He grabbed the binoculars, adjusted them slightly as he zoomed in, aware that Adeline was watching him. He could feel her gaze on him and it tested his focus.

Oh, hell. He stared hard at the man who'd arrived. "He's wearing a ball cap, but yeah, that's him. He just kissed her, she grabbed onto his shirt and tried to get him to stay." Karen had looked very whiny as she'd followed after him. "He's…" Mac swung the binos to the front of the restaurant, seeing if Hayward left. But the front door didn't open. "Call Lincoln."

Adeline already had her phone out before he'd finished speaking.

She put it on speaker and it rang once, twice, three times… Eventually it went to voicemail and she hung up. "Should I call 911?"

"No," he said after a long pause. "I don't know if Harlan's father has contacts with the sheriff's department. And those lines are all recorded. I don't want anyone knowing we're here. If Hayward does have contacts or someone who's friends with his father and tells him we're here…" It wasn't worth the risk of putting his brothers and Adeline in danger any more than they already were. "Right now I only trust Lincoln."

"I'll try again," she said. This time it went straight to voicemail without even ringing. Either Lincoln didn't have service or he'd turned off his phone. She set hers down on the center console and looked over at Mac. "I could call Autumn." He could hear the hesitation in her tone. Before he could respond, Adeline called her friend, then cursed as she set her phone down. "It's Friday. She's teaching a class tonight. Of course she's not answering."

"We should follow him," Dylan said from the back.

"He's not going anywhere..." Mac cursed as Harlan stepped out the front door of the restaurant, his girlfriend trailing after him. Never mind, apparently he was leaving.

"What is it?" Joe asked.

"I spoke too soon. They're in the parking lot." Harlan pressed his girlfriend up against a car and kissed her hard. Then he stepped back and... "She grabbed something from her car and gave it to him." And now Harlan was getting into a vehicle. *Damn it.*

"What was it?" Adeline asked.

"A small bag."

"Let's follow him." Her tension rolled out in waves.

Mac knew he should say no, but he had experience with tailing people and...if he knew where Harlan was, it was a hell of a lot better than wondering whether the guy was going to attack them again. "Let's switch places."

He'd already turned off the dome light so he slid out of the passenger seat before she could argue, and from the way her lips had pursed together, he was pretty certain she'd planned to.

By the hood, he simply said, "I've got defensive driving experience."

Mac left his lights off as he pulled out of the parking lot, the acorns that had fallen on the hood while they'd sat there scattering under the movement.

He watched as Harlan made a right out of the parking lot, but instead of following immediately, he hung back.

"What are you doing?" Joe asked from the back.

"Just give me a second." Another vehicle pulled out after Harlan and headed in the same direction. Only then did Mac follow him. "I've got this."

"Is anyone else surprised that he's heading back to Verona Bay? He's got to know he has a warrant out for his arrest, but he's still hanging around," Adeline said.

Mac didn't like that at all. Harlan should be lying low and definitely not hanging out in Verona Bay, but here he was. None of it made sense.

"You're pretty good at this," Dylan said from the back, sounding impressed as Mac made another left turn.

Instead of following directly after him, Mac was using side streets to tail him. He was keeping Harlan in his line of sight without always being directly behind him. It was the best way to follow someone. No, the best way was to do it with a team and trade off but they only had one vehicle so this would have to do.

"Seriously," Adeline added. "Did you have another life as a spy or something?"

He snorted. "Or something." He'd had to do a hell of a lot of defensive driving in Afghanistan, and under much different circumstances.

"You plan on expanding on that?" Adeline asked.

"Maybe later." Mac followed Harlan's vehicle into a subdivision about a mile from their safe house.

A tingling started down his spine. Harlan was way too close to their safe house for comfort. When the guy turned down a dead-end street, Mac drove past it. He'd have to stop and follow him on foot. He snagged his phone as he parked along a darkened curb where one of the streetlights was busted.

"You three stay here," he ordered right before he jumped out. He'd learned that not giving them time to argue was key.

CHAPTER TWENTY-TWO

Harlan glanced around the quiet neighborhood, parking two houses down from his target in the quiet cul-de-sac. He'd gotten what he needed from Karen, for now, and hoped she'd come through for him. Hell, *she* better pray this information was good.

He knew that Ian had flipped on him, that pussy. And now he was going to die. Ian had been arrested, then miraculously let go. *Uh-uh. Hell no.* The bastard wasn't returning his calls either and he hadn't gone home.

But Harlan knew where he was, thanks to Karen.

As he reached the house, he hurried up the driveway and rounded the side of the house. At the side door, he could see into the garage.

Ian's piece of shit Pontiac sat there.

Adrenaline spiked inside him. This was it. He was fed up with people screwing him over. Tired of getting shit on.

He never should have gotten thrown in jail that first time. He'd been young and stupid, but since his dad had been a cop at the time—before he'd made it up to chief of police—the judge had decided to make an example of him.

Soon Harlan would go after that judge too. But that was a job for the future. He had more important ends to tie up right now.

Starting with... He grinned to himself as he found the hidden key tucked into a fake rock by a potted plant. Karen had told him he'd find it here. She'd been right. He was going to fuck her so good later.

The key slipped into the side garage door perfectly and his heart rate kicked up even higher. He slid on gloves before touching the doorknob, then glanced behind him as he opened and shut the door. The back of his neck tingled slightly, but it'd been like that since he'd heard about the arrest warrant. His father had told him about it, told him to turn himself in when he'd called asking for money.

All of a sudden he cared? Where had he been the last seventeen years? He should have gotten Harlan out of jail sooner, or made sure he didn't go at all. But no, he'd failed him too.

Another spike of rage slammed into his skull as he tried the key in the interior door that led to...a laundry room.

He slowly pulled out his pistol as he eased that door shut behind him and listened.

There was a TV going somewhere in the house. It wasn't that late so it made sense Ian would be up.

Not for long though.

The next door opened up into the kitchen. Karen had told him Ian was staying here; apparently it was owned by a woman Ian screwed occasionally. She and

Karen weren't tight, but they talked. She was out of town and had told Ian he could crash until she got back.

The door creaked as Harlan started to close it behind him and he winced. But there was no movement, no shuffling sounds, so he finished closing it. As he stepped farther into the kitchen, his eyes landed on the butcher block of knives.

They practically gleamed from the little night-light in the corner, calling his name, begging him to slide one out.

A red haze fell over his vision. Yes, a knife was better than a gun. Quieter. More personal.

More painful.

At the sound of flushing, Harlan grabbed the biggest knife, caressing the handle with his gloved hand. It was beautiful. Yeah, this would do the job just fine.

Footsteps were growing closer, coming down the hallway as Ian muttered to himself about something.

Moving quickly, Harlan opened the pantry door and slipped inside, not closing it all the way.

A few moments later the lights in the kitchen flickered on and there was Ian. Shirtless, in just a pair of boxers, he strode to the refrigerator and grabbed a beer. Then he pulled out the empty six-pack container and tossed it onto the counter before popping the top. He swayed slightly before he started chugging.

What any woman saw in Ian, Harlan didn't know. Ian had grown soft over the years, drank too much, didn't work out like they had when they'd been in high school.

Whereas Harlan had bulked up in prison, put on forty pounds of pure muscle. He'd also learned how to fight, to protect himself.

This wasn't going to be much of a fight unfortunately, but Ian had decided to put himself on Harlan's list by stabbing him in the back.

Now Harlan would stab him. There was some poetic justice in that.

As Ian started to leave the kitchen, Harlan silently stepped out of the pantry. The hinge made the slightest creaking sound and Ian turned. His dark eyes went wide but Harlan lunged, knife gripped tight.

He shoved it straight into Ian's chest, hard and fast. Ian's eyes went wide as the bottle slipped from his fingers, shattering on the pristine pale gray tile.

"This is for stabbing me in the back," he growled as he released the hilt and shoved Ian.

He fell, a muted sound emerging from his throat as he landed hard on the tile, his skull cracking against it. Blood and beer pooled together around him.

Harlan stared down at him, at the blood, watching it create a dark river away from Ian's dying body.

He stepped forward, slammed his boot on the blade once for good measure. It felt good, the way Ian's body gave, caved in.

Ian tried to suck in a breath as blood now poured out of his mouth. He just stared up in horror at Harlan, his hands flapping once in an attempt to pull the knife out. But just as quickly, they fell to his side as he gasped, drowning in his own blood.

His adrenaline spiked again as he watched the life fade from Ian's eyes.

As Ian continued gurgling, Harlan stepped over him and headed for the back door. He wouldn't be using the vehicle he'd come in and he wouldn't be leaving the same way.

That was two people down, and many more to go.

The world was going to learn that they didn't fuck with Harlan Hayward and get away with it. Next up was Mac Collins.

CHAPTER TWENTY-THREE

"Mac didn't give us any time to argue," Adeline murmured more to herself than his brothers. He'd just jumped out of the SUV and disappeared into the darkness.

"So what's up with you guys?" Joe asked from the back, clearly unconcerned.

But Adeline didn't like any of this, didn't like Mac going off on his own. It had been one thing to spy on Hayward's girlfriend with the knowledge that they had distance from her and weren't under direct threat from Hayward at the time. This...was different. Now Mac was by himself, something she hated. It didn't matter how capable he was, she was still worried for him.

"What do you mean?" She turned in her seat to look at Joe.

"You and Mac. Are you dating?"

Oh. Ah, she so did not want to talk about her and Mac with his younger brothers. Or anyone really. She turned away, glancing out at the quiet street. There were cars in most of the driveways, and more likely tucked away in garages, but not all homes had them. Some just had carports. Nearly every single home had Christmas lights up, some with lit-up animals in the front yards, and a couple Santas on roofs. "We're just friends."

"Yeah right," Dylan said. "You're good for him. You bring him out of his shell some. Sometimes he's too quiet, too introverted."

Stunned, she turned around to look at him. "Are *you* calling him introverted? You're normally so quiet."

He lifted a shoulder. "It's a different kind of quiet. I open up around people I like. Mac only opens up around us and a few friends. Barely. He keeps a lot of stuff close to the vest. He's different with you. He lets his guard down. When you're around, he's...the brother I remember before our parents died."

Oooh. She blinked, not knowing what to say. At all.

"Just don't break his heart," Joe added.

"Look guys, Mac and I are just friends." Yeah right, a little voice in her head challenged. There was heat between them, already at a boil and ready to spill over.

The brothers looked at each other, then immediately back at her. Seriously it was like they choreographed this stuff.

The driver's door jerked open suddenly and Adeline nearly jumped until she realized it was Mac. Thank God he was okay. That invisible weight on her chest lifted. "What happened?"

"He disappeared around the corner of a house at the end of the street. He didn't see me and I didn't see him go in, but he had to have. I don't like any of this. We've got to call 911."

He was already pulling his phone out, but her phone rang and it was Lincoln. She shoved it at Mac, who immediately answered.

"I'm with Adeline and my brothers," Mac said on speaker.

"Good. I'm sorry I couldn't call you back earlier. I've had a lot going on the last couple hours. Where are you now? Are you guys safe?"

"We're off Loch Ness Road." Mac's tone was neutral, but Adeline winced.

Lincoln cursed. "You're not at the rental?"

"No," Adeline started. "We tried to call you—"

"It doesn't matter. You guys need to get home and lock yourselves inside. I need you sitting tight. We've found a body…in the pond on his property. It's why I've been tied up." It went all muffled for a moment and then he said quietly, "This is off the record. But…it was someone close to Harlan. We've got a witness tying him to it. This is serious."

"You're sure he did it?" Mac asked, his voice tight.

"It's an open investigation."

Mac cursed low at the non-answer. "Look, we followed him. We've both tried calling you the last couple hours. I saw him go into a house right off Loch Ness Road. Or I saw him disappear behind the house, not technically go inside. But I know he doesn't live here."

"Stay where you are, but do not approach him if you see him!" Lincoln hung up.

Mac handed the phone to Adeline as he opened the front door once again and jumped out. He looked at her. "Get in the driver's seat, keep the engine running and don't let anyone but me inside. If you see someone approaching other than Lincoln, *drive*."

"Wait—" But he'd already closed the door. She growled to herself even as she slid over into the driver's seat.

"Holy hell," Joe said from the back.

She felt that she was in a tunnel as she gripped the steering wheel, the engine now running. "Joe, you watch the back, see if anyone approaches from behind. Dylan, you keep an eye on the sides of the vehicle. I'll watch the front. If anyone approaches, we're leaving. We'll head straight to where Mac ran off to." Because they sure as hell weren't leaving him behind.

Worry crept up her spine, knowing that he'd run into potential danger. He might be trained, but he was still human, could still get shot. The thought of something happening to Mac... She swallowed hard.

She couldn't go there.

CHAPTER TWENTY-FOUR

Lincoln raced down the residential street, his lights on, but he kept the siren off. As he turned onto Loch Ness, his lights swept over an SUV and...he spotted four people behind the tinted windows.

Someone jumped out of the front seat and he tensed, but that faded when he realized it was Mac.

He parked behind them, one of his deputies pulling in behind him. Before he'd gotten out, Adeline and Mac's brothers all poured out of the SUV. He couldn't *believe* they were here. And if he hadn't been out on Hayward's property hauling a body out of the water earlier, he'd have gotten their damn calls.

"There's a body inside." Mac's expression was grim. "I did my best not to disturb the scene but when you mentioned there'd been a murder... I saw Harlan near this house. I had to make sure someone wasn't in danger. But I was too late." Regret flashed in Mac's eyes.

"It's not your fault. Who knows how long it would've taken us to find out about this... Do you know who it is?" Lincoln was pretty sure he did but wanted to see if Mac had an identification.

"No. It's not pretty, fair warning."

Yeah, murder never was. "Stay here," he ordered. "I mean it. No one leaves. We're going to have to take statements from all of you." At least then he could keep an eye on all of them.

One of his deputies started talking to them as Lincoln hurried past the SUV and made his way into the house. The front door was slightly open and he needed to ask Mac if it had been open or if he'd left it that way. Weapon up, he swept the house like he normally would, circling back to the body in the kitchen.

Ian Shaw.

Hell. Lincoln bit back a curse. This never should have happened. And this all could've been prevented if he'd found Hayward.

But the bastard had been elusive. They'd had a tail on his girlfriend but she'd disappeared. His deputy thought she'd switched vehicles or had a friend pick her up downtown. Either way, as far as they knew, she was lying low too.

Slipping on gloves, he crouched down next to Ian, regret slicing through him. He checked his pulse even though there was no doubt Ian was dead. The butcher knife embedded deep in his chest and the pool of blood on the kitchen floor guaranteed that.

Damn it. Ian had told him he'd be getting out of town for a while so Lincoln had put him out of his mind for now, thinking he was safe.

"We've already started securing the house," Marisol said as she approached from behind.

Sighing, he stood and turned to face her. In uniform, she had on gloves too as she eyed Ian, her expression as grim as he felt.

"He's not going to stop," he said more to himself, but she nodded.

"A knife is personal." She cleared her throat. "He tried to shoot up Collins and Adeline but he stabs this guy? Yeah, he had to know about the statement Ian gave you."

Lincoln nodded, not liking any of it, but she was right. They'd filed paperwork at the courthouse and then somehow Harlan had found out about Ian turning on him. Someone had told him about this. And Harlan had multiple weapons that they knew of, given the different caliber bullets found at Mac's workshop. For some reason he'd chosen to go up close and personal for this. And he'd used a knife from on-site—the butcher knife was the only slot empty in the knife block—so while Lincoln wasn't one hundred percent sure, he was going with his instinct that Harlan had used the knife because he'd *wanted* to get his hands bloody, so to speak.

Guns were violent too, far too violent and far too often ended up in the wrong hands, but killing someone with a knife forced you to get close. It spoke of rage and hatred. Being out of control.

Fuuuck. This was just going to escalate until they brought him in.

"Keep securing the scene." He stepped back. "I need to talk to the witnesses."

"Why are they even here?" Marisol frowned as she started opening up the crime scene kit.

"A misguided attempt at helping," he murmured as he stalked past her. Or he assumed that was what had happened, given some of the messages he'd listened to on the way here.

The four of them were leaning against the outside of the SUV as he approached and he couldn't help but notice that Mac and Adeline were very close to each other. They weren't quite touching, but maybe an inch separated them. Mac's body was angled toward hers in a protective stance.

"I'm going to need an official statement from all of you. You're going to have to come down to the station and be interviewed separately. It's going to be a late night," Lincoln said, "because we're already dealing with a lot of shit right now. And I really want to know what the hell you were thinking." He focused on Mac now. Because he wouldn't have expected him to go off half-cocked, chasing down Hayward. Much less with Adeline and his brothers in tow.

Adeline stepped forward, putting her body in front of Mac's. "We ganged up on him. He didn't want to do this but I created a fake Instagram profile and found out where his girlfriend was going to be. So we drove to where she was and Hayward showed up. We followed him—though we did call and text you. We kept a decent distance and were never in danger."

He blinked at the dump of information. "You created a fake Instagram profile?"

"Of course. Hayward attacked us with a gun! He shot at us and burned down Mac's shop. And now he's running free. And apparently murdering people," she added, a bite to her words.

Mac put a comforting arm around her shoulders. She stilled immediately, some of her anger seeming to fade as she leaned into him.

"Look," Mac started, his tone completely neutral, "we shouldn't have followed him—probably shouldn't have left the house, and that's on me—but once we spotted him, and I couldn't get hold of you, I just couldn't let it go. I'm not sorry. Actually, I'm sorry I didn't follow the bastard into the house. I thought it was a safe house and he was holing up there."

Lincoln studied all four of them and sighed. Glancing over at one of his deputies, he waved them over. "I get it. But you guys are still going to have to make statements."

"Should we just head to the station?" Adeline asked.

"Yes, but I've got to split you up."

Adeline snorted. "If we wanted to get our stories straight, we were here for a while before you got here. There's no sense in splitting us up now."

Mac closed his eyes and sighed. "You're not supposed to say that out loud," he murmured.

"I'm just saying that if—"

Lincoln held up a hand, a low-grade headache starting at the base of his skull. "I know what you're saying. But I have to follow protocol. Mac, you can drive the SUV to the station. Joe and Dylan, get in the back of Shaughnessy's car. Adeline, you're riding with me. It's probably going to be a little while though. I've got to make sure everything is secure before we leave."

Grumbling under her breath, she nodded and crossed her arms over her chest.

"It's going to be okay," Mac said as he pulled her close. "We didn't do anything wrong—I mean it was stupid, but not wrong."

She nudged him with her elbow, her expression softening as she looked up at him. "Not stupid."

Lincoln pulled out his radio and responded to an inquiry from inside, stepping away from the four of them.

Tonight was definitely going to be a very long night. And it was going to get a hell of a lot worse if they didn't find Harlan, and soon.

CHAPTER TWENTY-FIVE

Adeline tapped her fingernail against the table in the interrogation room. It was a nervous tic, one she couldn't seem to stop. Her adrenaline from earlier had long since dissipated and now she was punchy and exhausted—and ready to go home.

"You've gotta stop doing that," Joe murmured, his eyes closed as he leaned back in one of the chairs.

Mac stood at the corner of the long table, arms over his chest and his back to the two-way mirror that lined one wall.

Dylan had actually draped himself across the table, his eyes closed as he tried to sleep, which was basically impossible under the sharp fluorescent lights. But he was giving it his best shot.

At least they'd already given their statements and the deputies on duty had brought them food and hot coffee.

Not that the caffeine had done much other than keep her warm. It was one in the morning and she was about ready to crash, and crash hard. But Lincoln had said he needed to talk to them before they left. That it was important.

As if her thoughts had summoned him, the door swung open. He swept his gaze over the four of them. "I'm sorry to keep you guys waiting. We had one of the relatives of the victims arrive and..." He cleared his throat. "Anyway, I want to run something by you." He focused on Mac and Adeline now, his expression dark.

"No." There was no give in that one word as Mac subtly stepped half in front of Adeline, as if protecting her from something.

She touched his forearm gently. "He hasn't even said what he wants."

"I can tell I'm not going to like it."

Dylan groaned and shoved up from the table, looking younger than normal as he pushed his messy hair out of his face. "I'm ready to get home."

"Your *rental* home," Lincoln clarified, no room for argument in his tone.

Mac simply nodded because yeah, that was where they were going.

"Can I finish?" Lincoln gave Mac a sharp look.

Mac just nodded.

"I have an idea for setting Harlan up," he started. "One that will not put you in any danger. But it will involve you on the fringes as we bait him."

"Nope," Mac snarled, moving in front of her lightning fast, fully blocking her.

She blinked, surprised by how quickly he'd shifted from his casual pose to completely blocking her view of the sheriff. She placed a hand on his back but he didn't move. Tension vibrated through him, all his muscles taut. "Mac, let's at least listen to him."

"We're not going to be bait. *Adeline* is not going to be bait."

"Look," Lincoln snapped, "I've got two dead bodies and no doubt that the count is just going to go up. So listen until I'm done. It's not a stretch to think you and Adeline are a couple. I was thinking that you could stop at a few shops tomorrow—today—show your faces around town and then drop the information to some friends that you're going to be getting away to one of the cabins over at that RV park. You know the one, it's got cabin rentals up there now. You wouldn't actually be doing that, just telling people that you are. There's a good chance this will get back to Harlan, and if he takes the bait, we'll be waiting for him—with you two nowhere nearby. Not even in the same zip code. I just need you to help spread the gossip in an organic way so he believes it." Lincoln was silent for a long moment when they didn't respond. "He may figure out that it's a lie but it's a good plan. One I can't pull off without your help."

"What the hell?" Mac finally growled. "I don't like any of this." He shifted slightly, as if trying to block her again as he did that protective stance thing.

"He's not going to attack us in the middle of town," she said. She didn't like it either, but it was a really good plan. "He's not going to be in the middle of town on a Saturday. He's hiding right now. There's a warrant out for his arrest and he knows it. Right?" She looked around him at Lincoln who simply nodded.

Mac's expression remained grim.

"I'm not just going to leave you guys alone to your own devices. I'll have all my people watching you, but covertly. You could stop at Bianca's coffee shop, maybe the quilt shop, and one other place. Just talk casually to a couple friends and then word will spread fast. Let's make the third stop the diner. Everyone will know about you guys after that. And I'll have people at each store already in place so you're never not protected."

"It's not a terrible idea," she murmured, which just earned her a growl from Mac.

"I can't believe you're agreeing to this so quickly."

"It's a good idea—a damn good one," Lincoln said, drawing Mac's attention back to him. "And we've had two murders within days of each other. Harlan isn't stopping. He's going to kill as many people as he can before he's arrested. And I'm not going to let that happen. We're a small town with small resources, and if I can actually bait him into coming to me... I can't lose any more people."

"Fine," Mac snapped out. "We'll work out the details later. Right now, we're going to get some sleep. One of us will call you in the morning...if you answer," he added testily, glaring at Lincoln.

Adeline figured he was only agreeing but didn't actually plan to go through with it. He was too keyed up, too...something. Mac motioned to his brothers and then tucked her up against him, wrapping his arm around her shoulders tight.

She actually liked Lincoln's idea and she didn't think he'd ever put her in danger. But Mac wasn't thinking about any of that right now. He was very likely thinking about the body he'd found earlier.

Sighing, she leaned into him as he hustled her out. He was so warm, smelled so good, and she was so damn tired. For five minutes she was going to not worry about what tomorrow would bring.

"I'll call you around eight," Lincoln called out.

Mac simply grunted in response.

CHAPTER TWENTY-SIX

"What are you doing here?" Chief of Police Robert Hayward frowned at Lincoln, his gaze trailing past him to the trio of sheriff's deputies lining the walkway up to his two-story Craftsman-style house.

"I've got a warrant to search your house." Lincoln held it up, handed him a copy and waited for the man to scan it. Hayward was more than familiar with these, but Lincoln was trying to show him some courtesy even if the guy didn't deserve it. "As you can see, we're searching for your son and—"

"I know what the hell this says! You could've just asked. You didn't need a damn warrant," he spat.

Lincoln could see the rage burning in the man's eyes, and knew that if it had just been the two of them, Hayward would have decked him. Or attempted to, anyway. The guy was softer since the last time Lincoln had seen him, not as in-shape as he'd once been. Though he was still built like a bull, his shoulders broad and his arms muscular. His hair had gone fully gray now and it peppered his short beard as well.

"I'm just following procedure." Lincoln kept his voice neutral, wanting the situation to remain as calm as possible. "We're simply looking for your son." He held up a hand, motioned for his deputies to head inside.

"Well, just wait a minute, my wife is having breakfast—"

"One of my deputies will escort her outside." He motioned to Marisol, who kept walking right past both of them.

"I bet you just love this, don't you?" Hayward growled.

"Why would I love this?" He stared at the older man. "I *hate* doing this. Hate being here. Hate everything about this. But your son is wanted for at least two murders. And I'm not going to let him kill anyone else. If you know where he is, you need to tell me before he hurts someone else. Because he is absolutely not done killing," Lincoln snapped.

"My son didn't do anything," Hayward snarled, but it was clear he didn't believe his own words.

"Bobby, what's going on?" In her robe, her brown hair peppered with gray down around her shoulders, his petite wife strode out the front door with Marisol at her side. She looked between him and Lincoln, confusion in her blue eyes.

"It's all just a misunderstanding," Hayward said.

She turned to Lincoln then, her eyes beseeching. They'd met a few times before and he'd always liked Betty. "Sheriff, what are you doing here? Why are you all searching our house? I don't understand this." She clutched the edge of her robe, tension bracketing her mouth.

"Ma'am—"

"Don't you talk to my wife!" Hayward snarled and gripped his wife by the arm, practically dragging her across the front patio as he angrily whispered in her ear.

The two of them spoke in quiet tones as his deputies entered the house. Lincoln didn't think Harlan was here but they had to do their due diligence. Had to cover all their bases, and in another two hours he would start their sting operation with Mac and Adeline. Though Mac was still pissed about the whole thing, at least he was agreeing to it.

It was impossible to know if it would work, but it was a good idea and he knew that SWAT teams in bigger cities often employed similar tactics. Not exactly the same, but they utilized what they had when they needed to draw people out of hiding.

And he had faith in his deputies' abilities to keep Adeline and Mac safe while strolling through town pretending to be a couple.

Though he wasn't sure how much pretending was actually going on at this point.

Twenty minutes later his people stepped outside, all nodding at him as they headed back to their cars. It was as he'd thought, Harlan wasn't here. But chances were high he'd hear about this and Lincoln hoped it helped him make the decision to surrender. He didn't actually think it would, but he was hopeful.

"If you know where your son is, you need to tell us," Lincoln said to both of the Haywards as he stepped down one of the stairs. "I want to bring him in alive." So justice could be served and the victims of his crimes would see him get life.

"You're full of shit, sheriff. You don't care about him," Robert snapped.

"I care that two people are dead. I care that his fingerprints were at one of the murder scenes. And we have a witness who saw him entering the house at the time of the second murder," he said, his gaze on Hayward's wife now. She sucked in a breath at his last statement. Lincoln wasn't talking for Hayward's benefit anymore, but for Betty's. If he could get through to her, maybe get her to give up her son's location, they could avoid any more bloodshed. "We're going to catch him, but it'll be so much easier if we do it quickly and quietly." Without waiting for a response, he turned on his heel even as Hayward shouted behind him.

"You're going to pay for this! You're going to hear from my lawyer. I'll sue you personally!"

Ignoring the empty threats, Lincoln slid into the front of his car and kicked it into gear, scanning the surrounding property as he left. He'd already alerted all adjacent counties of Harlan's arrest warrant and it was at the point he had to let the local news know about him too. He wanted people to be on the lookout for him—but not to approach.

Now he had to get ready for the morning's op. He'd already gone over everything with Mac and Adeline a couple hours ago. The two had sounded exhausted, having only a few hours of sleep, but they were both ready to get this over with.

He understood—they wanted to get their lives back. And he *wanted* them to get their lives back too. To be able to live in safety without worrying a meth-dealing asshole was waiting in the shadows to kill them.

As he headed down the road, his cell phone rang, Autumn's ringtone filling the car.

For just a moment, the tension in his shoulders eased. Everything else faded away as he answered.

Because no matter how bad things were today, he had Autumn in his life, a baby on the way, and soon he would be proposing.

He just hoped she said yes.

CHAPTER TWENTY-SEVEN

"Still don't like this," Mac grumbled as they stepped into Sweet Spot, Bianca's café, holding hands. They'd already gotten a few curious looks from the moment they'd parked down the street and walked here hand in hand.

"And *I* can't believe you're still saying the same thing." Adeline squeezed his hand and looked up at him with a warm smile. "We're *supposed* to be a couple in love." Her words were quiet, so only he could hear. She knew that one of Lincoln's deputies or maybe one of his detectives was already here, having come in earlier to stake out the place.

Lincoln had set up his deputies in various shops around town, all the locations on Main Street that Mac and Adeline had on their itinerary to stop at. It was much easier to have them in place already, as opposed to following them and being obvious. And then when she and Mac were done with their little show, they would be heading straight out of town and getting into a different vehicle. Then they would loop back to Mac's rental where his brothers and one of Lincoln's deputies were waiting.

The plan was perfect. But Mac didn't like being out in the open with her regardless.

Mac's eyes flared with heat, maybe at her words, she wasn't sure. Everything sort of funneled out around her when he looked down at her like that. She knew they were acting, but it didn't seem to matter.

Taking her off guard, he slid his hand along her cheek, cupping it oh so gently as he rubbed his thumb over her skin. Then he leaned down and kissed her...on the forehead. Okay, that was a bit disappointing. Still, tingles blossomed inside her at his closeness. Probably better he hadn't kissed her on the mouth because she was liable to just jump him right here.

"Come on," he murmured, nudging her forward, and she realized they were holding up the line.

She blinked and also realized that a few customers were staring. So was Bianca from behind the countertop. Her eyes were wide as she slid change across to the woman in front of the cash register.

Adeline had told Bianca about them coming up here—about everything. But it was still likely a shock to her friend to *see* the two of them together, actually acting like a couple.

The line moved quickly, with Bianca and one of her employees working like bees, taking orders and making drinks at an impressively rapid pace. By the time they got to the front, Bianca had a grin on her face. "I guess I don't have to ban you after all," she said to Mac.

He frowned. "Ban me?"

"She's joking," Adeline said, sliding her arm around Mac's waist. At this point she was weak in the knees and could admit it. But come on, he'd put his lips on her fore-head—how could she not be weak? *Gah.* This was beyond ridiculous. *She* was ridiculous.

A low buzz of fear still hummed inside her, a worry that Harlan would somehow find them and jump out at them like the boogeyman. But she simply couldn't see that happening. It was when they finally left downtown that Adeline knew her fear would really spike.

As it was, she was currently half wrapped around the sexiest, sweetest and, okay, most ripped guy she'd ever known. Not to mention he was a good brother, a father figure to said brothers, and had been trying to protect her when he'd blown her off. Things between them were weird right now, but it didn't change her growing feelings for him.

"I know what you want to drink, Adeline. So how about some scones and cannoli as well?"

Adeline grinned, hoping she was hiding her tension. "You know me so well."

"And throw in some blueberry pastries, strawberry pastries and a couple macaroons," Mac added, pulling his wallet out.

"Hungry?" Adeline asked.

"Gotta keep up our strength," Mac said just a little too loudly.

Oooohhhh God. She felt her cheeks flush, knowing what people would think. Which was of course the whole point of this farce. They had to sell that they were a real couple, and sell it good.

"So how have things been since you got back?" Bianca's voice was normal enough, though she'd raised it slightly, hoping to be overheard.

"We got back safely after all that flooding, but since our getaway was interrupted we're going to take another trip up to Crescent Lake," Adeline said.

"That's a great place to get away. You'll have plenty of privacy."

Adeline was glad she'd warned Bianca about this earlier; it would help sell things for them around town. Enough people had overheard that soon gossip would spread like kudzu.

They chatted for a few more minutes, then Mac paid and they took their steaming coffees and bag of pastries outside.

"Let's sit here," he murmured, motioning her to one of the benches along the sidewalk. Everything was decorated for Christmas, an explosion of red and gold lights all over Main Street. And all the shops downtown, including Tailwaggers, had light displays in each window. It was like something out of a movie, but it was hard to enjoy knowing that Harlan was out there, somewhere.

She hoped this was successful, that the gossip mill was already working in their favor. "Why?" She sat next to him as he wrapped his arm around her shoulder and cuddled her close.

She knew this was all acting for him but she still liked it, still liked being held by him. He made her feel safe and...happy. The holidays were always hard, but this year things had been different. Even with all the insanity of what they were dealing with, she felt...a lot less alone. And it was all because of the very sexy lumberjack-looking man right next to her.

"This is Main Street. Do you know how many people are going to see us as they drive by?" Turning his body so that he was angled more toward her, he cupped her cheek again, tilting her head up toward his. "For the record," he murmured, his gorgeous lips just inches from her mouth, "this is not how I envisioned our first kiss."

Wait, he'd envisioned their first kiss? She wondered if he'd obsessed about it like she had, then her brain went on the fritz as his lips brushed over hers.

It was just the briefest, barest skating touch, their lips sweeping against each other when he started to pull back.

But something came over her, possession maybe, and she leaned forward, nipping his bottom lip between her teeth.

He let out a low growl and took over in an instant, sliding his hand back and cupping the back of her head as he flicked his tongue against her. A burst of heat exploded inside her at his taste, his touch, everything.

They both pulled apart as if he'd also realized how quickly things were heating up.

"Good thing I have this bag." His tone was dry as he situated the pastry bag over his crotch.

It took her a moment to realize what he meant before a burst of laughter escaped. So he was turned on.

The kiss had affected him as much as her. That...definitely mattered to her. She wanted him and he wanted her.

She couldn't think of a single thing to say to that, so she leaned her head on his shoulder and took a sip of her drink as they watched cars and people pass along the street. Even as she tried to relax, she couldn't help but look for Harlan. It felt insane that he would be anywhere near downtown Verona Bay when there was a warrant out for him, but her eyes tracked faces nonetheless.

Mac squeezed her shoulder once. "Don't look so glum. We've got to be a happy couple."

"I know," she murmured. Things felt very different now and she wondered what would happen once they got back to the rental. Were things *different* between them?

Even if he was physically attracted to her, it didn't necessarily mean he wanted something along the lines of a relationship. He had before, but then things had gotten all crazy.

She shoved all those thoughts out of her mind and watched the happy shoppers across the street, bags and coffees in hand, talking and laughing as they prepared for the holiday. They were all just living their lives, and she and Mac were hoping to draw out a killer.

A few people stopped and talked to them while they drank their coffee, and after about ten minutes he said, "Let's go to the quilt shop."

"Fair warning, you're going to be bombarded by some of my friends. Or you very likely will be. They're on a mission to make everyone into quilters."

"I don't mind." Then he grinned at her, a slow, unfurling one that sent ribbons straight to her core. Oh...she was in so much trouble where Mac was concerned.

So, so, much trouble. Because she was not acting right now.

* * *

"I think we stopped at enough places," Adeline said as Mac drove down Main Street later, heading out of downtown. She'd liked everyone thinking they were together. Part of her wished that they were. After that kiss, she'd let her mind run wild but Mac was sooo hard to read.

"Definitely." He glanced in the rearview mirror as he turned down a side street. "I just want to say for the record that I still don't like that you were out in the open like this."

"You want this guy caught. And you were out in the open too."

He lifted a broad shoulder, his muscles pulled taut as he gripped the steering wheel. "I'm not worried about myself."

That seemed like such a typically male thing to say. Or maybe it was typical Mac. She didn't know him well enough.

Her phone rang before she could say anything. She answered immediately. "I've got you on speaker," she said.

"You guys did great and no one is tailing you," Lincoln said. "I'm in an unmarked vehicle and staying back a ways, but I'm not seeing anyone behind you."

"I thought I saw him downtown," Mac said abruptly.

Adeline shifted against her seat, looking at him in surprise. He hadn't said anything, hadn't let on at all. Her heart rate kicked up.

"I didn't say anything because I didn't want you to react," he said as if he'd read her mind. Or maybe just her body language.

"I got your text," Lincoln said, so clearly he'd told Lincoln.

She frowned, annoyed Mac hadn't said a word to her. "And?"

"I had one of my guys head in the direction you told me," Lincoln said. "But there was a mugging and he had to stop it. We didn't see him anywhere."

"I think it was my imagination getting away with me anyway," Mac murmured. "There was no sane reason for Harlan to be downtown, not walking around a bunch of people. How's the investigation going?"

"It's going." Lincoln's tone was tired. "He must have ditched his cell phone and there have been no movements on his credit card. He's definitely lying low. If I had to guess, someone's provided him a place to crash and is giving him money."

"You probably can't answer, but has he reached out to his parents?"

There was a long pause. "Not that we can tell."

"We're almost to the drop-off spot," Mac said.

They were going to drop off this vehicle and then pick up another one and head back into town to the rental where his brothers were waiting for them.

"I just confirmed with my deputy. He's waiting for you guys. I'll take care of the vehicle you're in now and stash it at the cabins. It'll help sell that you two are vacationing there."

"So now it's just a waiting game?" Adeline asked, her nerves fraying.

"It is for you guys. I want you to *promise* you're not going to leave the house this time. I don't have enough manpower to watch your place full-time. If I do, it'll tie up resources I could be using to hunt him down. I've got someone who's going to be doing steady drive-bys of the area, however."

"We're not going anywhere. If she tries to leave, I'll tie her up." Mac shot her a look that was probably meant to be all firm and intense, but damn, she kind of liked the thought of him tying her up. But only if he did hot things to her.

Gah, she had to stop. She had way too much else on her mind. Still... Heat rushed to her cheeks at her wayward thoughts and she was glad he was now watching the road and not her.

Lincoln simply snorted. "Good enough for me. Keep your lines open in case I need to reach you."

After they disconnected, she leaned back against the seat, though a ball of tension had settled deep inside her. "He might not fall for this trap."

"True. But they'll catch him. Harlan doesn't have enough money or brains to go on the run long-term. He could probably disappear for a little while, but he's going to trip up. He's going to get stupid and then he'll get caught."

"Yeah, but how many people will he hurt in the meantime?"

Mac's expression darkened as he turned back to face the road. "I know. I'm worried about that too. But my main concern is keeping you and my brothers safe."

She reached out and squeezed his leg. "And we will keep you safe." Someone had to look out for him.

Okay, she definitely saw heat in his gaze now. But he averted it just as quickly and turned on the radio.

There was no doubt that something was simmering between them, and once they were alone... Hell, it didn't matter. They had more to worry about than stupid hormones.

CHAPTER TWENTY-EIGHT

Harlan kept his hooded jacket pulled up over his head and a scarf wrapped around the bottom half of his face, not making him look out of the ordinary, considering how cold it was out today. Well, cold for Florida. Everyone was bundled up in hats, scarves and even boots. No flip-flops in sight.

He strode down Main Street in Verona Bay, blending in with the crowd of shoppers, his gaze snagging on Mac Collins and the bitch with him. One of his guys had texted him and told him that they thought they'd spotted Collins downtown.

He'd thought for sure that loser was holed up somewhere, *afraid*. He'd set Collins's place on fire and here the asshole was out shopping with someone. She was hot but... This could *not* stand.

Because he *knew* Collins had blown up his meth lab. He couldn't prove it but he'd followed the tracks back through the woods in the direction of Collins's house. And no one had taken credit for it—no one else would be stupid enough to cross him. It had to be him. And even if it wasn't, he blamed Collins for getting him locked up all those years ago, so he was still going to gut the bastard.

Harlan had been so pissed back then that his girl-friend had been cheating on him that he'd gone out and gotten wasted...and decided to rob a local bar. He shouldn't have roughed up the owner but he'd been so pissed and drunk, so they'd added assault and battery charges. He wouldn't have done any of that if not for Collins and that other bitch.

He took a breath, forcing his rage back as best he could. He had to be smart. He knew in the end he wasn't going to make it out of this alive. That was storybook shit. Eventually the Feds or someone would catch up with him. But he was going to take out as many people as possible before he died.

When he got out of prison, he'd started making real money, hadn't even thought of Collins in years. But then that hometown hero decided to blow up what's his? Cut into his profit?

Hell no. He had to make an example.

After killing his former partner, he'd decided to go after everyone who had ever wronged him. Then Ian had narced on him, so he'd killed him too.

He was stronger now, smarter. Something his father had never appreciated. God, he'd always pushed him too hard, tried to get him to be something he wasn't. Quickly he shelved thoughts of his father or he'd get off track.

It was easy to hide in plain sight here, and the stupid sheriff in charge could suck his dick. He wasn't afraid of that guy either. He might go after that bastard too for hassling his parents, for making his mom cry.

Harlan shoved his hands in his pockets and stopped at the next crosswalk with a group of teenage girls.

He raked his gaze over one of them, checking out her tight ass. *Damn.* Then he jerked his gaze forward when he noticed the older woman next to him frowning at him.

When the crosswalk turned go, he moved along with everyone else. Once he reached the other side, he saw that Mac and the Rodriguez woman were standing instead of sitting at that bench, heading in the opposite direction.

Though he didn't want to follow and end up getting caught, a compulsion compelled him to follow. After that smug Mac Collins.

Harlan gritted his teeth, forcing himself not to do something stupid like pull out his weapon and shoot the bastard right here in front of all these witnesses. If he did, he wouldn't be able to finish his list, finish killing every person who'd wronged him.

As he walked he pulled his cell phone out and pretended to look at it. It allowed him to keep his head down and not make eye contact with anyone. He was wearing sunglasses anyway but still. *Blend.* That was all he had to do while he kept tabs on Collins.

As he pretended to play on his phone, a text message popped up.

Saw the sheriff near the hardware store. In plain clothes, but it's him for sure.

His heart rate increased. A couple of his guys were downtown keeping a lookout for law enforcement.

This was his cue to leave. Instead of heading straight, he made a left at the next street as he texted back Elias. *Keep an eye on the happy couple if possible.* His crew knew that he suspected Mac had blown up the meth lab and they wanted revenge too. Because right now they didn't have any income. Or drugs. He never touched the stuff, knew how stupid it could make you, but he loved the money it brought in.

The crowd started to thin as he crossed another street. And as he reached another crosswalk, his girlfriend pulled up in her car.

"Get in," she said before rolling the window up.

He jumped into the back seat, glancing around as he shut the door behind him. "What are you doing?" He hadn't told her he'd be downtown. Hadn't told her anything about his whereabouts. He'd shown up to see her last night—to get some weapons he'd stashed with her. He'd thought about staying, but she'd been busy with friends and he'd had shit to take care of anyway.

"I was downtown shopping and saw you." She popped her gum, a habit that was slowly starting to annoy him.

But as her words registered, ice sliced through him. "You recognized me?"

"Only because I gave you that jacket." She turned on her blinker as she pulled up to a stop sign.

He relaxed at that, still glancing around for any threat. They weren't being followed. "You shouldn't be here." Though he could go for an easy lay.

"Neither should you." She gave him a hard look in the rearview mirror. With no sunglasses on, her blue eyes were sharp, annoyed. "You need to lie low, maybe get out of town. You're on the freaking news, wanted for murder."

He noticed that she didn't ask him if he did it. Because he didn't think she cared one way or another. Her father had been a lifelong criminal, had been sent up so many times, with his last stint in jail being the final one. He'd died inside and Karen hadn't shed a tear. She could be cold sometimes—and he liked it. She was also hot as hell. With thick, long, dark brown hair, big tits and a tight ass to hold on to, she was always down to get naked.

"I don't want you getting in any trouble."

He wasn't sure if she meant it, could never tell with her. She was so damn hot and cold, all over him, whiny and needy, then pushing him away the next second. "I can take care of myself." He'd been doing it for a long damn time.

She sniffed slightly before making another turn and heading straight out of town. "I saw that Collins guy that you hate," she said casually. "He was with that chick who runs the pet shop. A place for pet grooming," she muttered in disgust. "People really will spend all sorts of money on their damn dogs. It's ridiculous." She sniffed slightly again and he didn't know if it was from the cold or her growing coke problem.

When she pulled into the empty parking lot of the church, he frowned, tensing. He sure as hell wasn't going into any church. "What the hell are you doing?"

She knew where he was staying, a cabin on the outskirts of town. The place sucked, had barely working electricity, but it was somewhere to lay his head at night.

At least until he finished with his list. And Collins was next, along with the Rodriguez woman. Though he might have some fun with her before he killed her. And he was going to kill Collins's younger brothers too. But he'd make Collins watch that. He needed to suffer for being such a piece of shit.

"Who knows when I'll see you again," Karen murmured as she shoved the car into park.

He looked around and the parking lot was definitely empty. Thick oak trees blocked her car from the road. And from where she'd stopped, they would have a good view of anyone approaching. "Come on, I need to get back to the cabin. There are some things I need to take care of." He'd already texted one of his guys, telling them to bring his ride back to him there.

She completely ignored him and crawled into the back seat. That was when he saw that she had on a little skirt and thigh-high tights. And when she lifted up her skirt to straddle him, he realized she wasn't wearing anything underneath.

Just like that his dick was hard. She'd been downtown like that, no underwear, just walking around. Fuuuuccck him.

She rubbed a hand over his growing erection, the lust in her eyes white-hot as she quickly unzipped his pants.

He grabbed a condom but she tore it from his hands, ripped it open and quickly sheathed him in a practiced motion.

And then he was inside her.

Harlan groaned, clutching onto her hips. She really was a good fuck, always wet and ready for him. He shoved up her sweater, then tugged her bra down, wanting to see her breasts.

As she started riding him, he focused on the way her breasts bounced up and down even as thoughts of revenge filled him.

He was definitely going to take his sweet time with Mac's woman. And at that thought, he came hard inside his girlfriend, grunting against her neck as he did.

She grumbled something about him not waiting for her to get off but he didn't care.

He had shit to do.

CHAPTER TWENTY-NINE

"Might have some movement on the south perimeter." Gordon's voice came over the radio.

Lincoln barely moved the curtain of the cabin he and two other deputies were currently holed up in. Mac and Adeline had spread the news around town that they'd be here, and by this point Harlan had to have heard about it. He either showed up in the next couple days or he didn't.

"What do you see?" Lincoln murmured.

There were twelve cabins in total, six facing the other six with a long drive in between. They'd staged the entire area, with Mac's vehicle in front of one—the one he was currently in. And there were a few other cars parked randomly at some of the cabins, with camp chairs set up in front of them and towels hung up on the porches. Never mind that it was winter, there was a heated pool at the connected campsite about a mile away, so they were making this look as real as possible. And one wrong thing could tip off Harlan that this was a setup.

He'd pulled in some extra help with a neighboring police department so they could secure the entire perimeter. Otherwise he simply didn't have enough people, not to handle the entire county. Lincoln didn't want Harlan showing up and then escaping because he'd been short on manpower.

"I'm not sure yet. Maybe deer moving through." Gordon's voice was low.

"Keep me informed."

Lincoln hated this, hated that it was basically a waiting game. There were multiple alerts out on Harlan and the local news had run a segment, flashing his picture over multiple airings, so he knew they were going to find him. But he didn't want anyone else hurt before that happened. And even though Harlan was a piece of crap, he wanted him arrested and back in jail. Not dead. Unfortunately, he had a feeling Harlan would try to go out in a "suicide by cop" fashion. He didn't have anything to lose at this point—and that made him even more dangerous.

Harlan deserved to do time for his crimes, and the families of his victims needed to see that he was paying for them. Lincoln wanted to help give them the closure they deserved and make his town safe. And going back to prison for a man like that would be worse than death.

His phone buzzed in his pocket and he frowned when he saw the name on the screen. *What the hell?*

"Keep an eye on the window," he murmured to Nathan and Marisol as he stepped back and answered. "Sheriff Jordan here." He kept his voice low.

"Where are you on the investigation into my son?" Robert Hayward asked—or rather, demanded.

"You know I can't talk about an open investigation."

"What about the investigation you've opened into me?"

Lincoln winced. He'd kept that quiet, hadn't even had much of a chance to dig into Hayward. Not with the manhunt for the guy's son going on. Everything else non-priority had taken a back seat. "Chief, now is not the time for this. You know we're trying to locate your son. I'm going to reiterate what I said before. If you can help me with that, good. If not, I'm going to end this call."

"You're just a holier than thou asshole—"

Lincoln hung up. He wasn't going to listen to any crap from Hayward, but he made a note of it and would put it in his report later.

"Was that Hayward...ah, the chief?" Marisol asked.

"Yep."

She snorted and shook her head before turning back to the window. "I thought so. He's got such a loud voice. He's got to be scared if he's calling you."

Lincoln nodded, even though she'd turned around. Scared could be a good thing, but scared people often did very, *very* stupid things as well. And that bothered Lincoln. But he focused on the here and now. He had to keep his head on straight because his people's lives depended on him making smart decisions.

"I definitely got movement," Gordon murmured again.

"Location?"

"Cabin H. About twenty yards to the southwest of it. There's way too much movement in the bushes. I'm heading in."

"I've got your six." He slid his radio into the holster and turned to the others. "You guys stay here."

Lincoln slipped out the back door instead of the front and took the long way around, sticking to the shadows. Woods surrounded the cabins at the back of both rows, so it was easy enough to remain hidden. He checked in with his people as he hurried, letting them know it was him.

By the time he made it around to the correct cabin, he quietly radioed Gordon. "I'm directly by Cabin H." And he heard the rustling. "We head in that direction at the same time. You come in from the left, I take the right. Weapons up but try to bring him in alive. I want no loss of life tonight."

"Ten-four."

Moving quietly and quickly, they fanned in an outward circular motion. The closer they got, the louder the rustling grew. This could be anything, including a distraction, so his attention was high.

Weapon up, he ducked behind an oak tree, using it as cover. Then he eased around it and...

Lincoln jerked to a halt and lowered his weapon. A young couple were stretched out on a big quilted picnic blanket, going at it right next to an azalea bush. The man had her pinned underneath him and those were sounds of pleasure coming from her.

"Shit," he muttered.

Gordon, now directly across from him, snorted as he half glanced away, giving them privacy.

The couple jerked apart, finally realizing they weren't alone. The woman let out a short scream.

"What the hell!" The man—or college-age kid really—shouted in alarm. Fumbling, he grabbed the woman's shirt and shoved it in front of her in an effort to protect her modesty.

Lincoln looked away as well. He doubted this was some elaborate setup from Harlan. "What are you two doing out here? It's after dark and it's freezing."

"We're camping over in Crescent Lake RV Park. We just stepped away for a little bit while everyone's roasting marshmallows. We told my parents we were going hiking," the girl said sheepishly as she tugged her sweater into place.

"You might want to pick some of the leaves out of your hair before you head back." He looked at Gordon and jerked his chin. "Escort them to the RV park."

"No way!" the guy started. "My parents are going to—"

Lincoln fixed the guy with a hard stare. "I don't care about your parents. There is potentially a dangerous, armed individual in the woods right now. Stop arguing and let my deputy escort you."

The couple straightened and nodded, looking younger than he'd thought originally. Freaking teenagers.

As they and Gordon headed down the makeshift path in the direction of the park, Lincoln got on the radio and relayed what had happened. As he started back the way he'd come, there was a faint rumble in the air.

He paused, listening. It was an engine. And he knew it didn't belong to any of his people. Everyone was in place already. And no one would be driving around.

"A pickup truck is rolling up," Haskins murmured into his radio. "I'm letting it pass through. I see at least two people inside but it's too dark to tell for sure."

"Everyone hold position."

He didn't have time to get to the cabin he'd been in, so he jumped up on the back porch of Cabin G and opened the door. The owners had given them free access to use their cabins since they didn't have any renters at the moment. No one came out to the cabins in the winter, though they did use the RV hookups.

He kept the lights off, letting the faint illumination from outside the windows guide the way to the front of the cabin. His boots made little thuds as he hurried to the front window. As he peered out, sure enough, a two-door Toyota truck was rolling down the dirt road toward the primitive cabins. Instead of continuing down the road between the cabins, however, the truck veered off and disappeared into the woods. There was nowhere to go in that direction, so whoever was driving had to be parking.

He didn't think it was teenagers looking for a good time. He gently cracked one of the windows open and heard what definitely sounded like doors shutting.

Less than five minutes later two shadows appeared in the distance. There wasn't much light, except from a couple of the cabins they'd set up. A radio played in the distance from one of them, adding to the illusion that all was normal.

The two shadows moved out from behind the cabin and toward Mac's vehicle. Light from a nearby window faintly illuminated them enough to reveal them as men. Bulky jackets, boots, and ball caps. One of the men peered inside the parked vehicle. Then he nodded at the other one. The second guy hurried around the back while the first one eased up the front steps of the patio.

Lincoln waited while the man picked the lock and then radioed to the team that they were going in hot. Once the guy disappeared inside, Lincoln threw open the front door of his cabin and raced in the direction of the other one, his weapon up.

Three of his deputies converged on it with him, and two more were out back. Pulling out a flash-bang, he tossed it through the partially open door.

Two shouts of alarm filled the interior as it exploded. Lincoln raced up the stairs and kicked the door fully open.

"Fuck you," one of them shouted and rushed at Lincoln, his gait unsteady.

Lincoln sidestepped, stuck his foot out and tripped the guy. As he did, he swiveled and slammed him fully on the ground, securing his arms behind his back. As he snapped the cuffs into place he was vaguely aware of Marisol doing the same to the second suspect.

"Get the hell off me," the man snarled as Lincoln hauled him to his feet. When he got a good look at him, he realized it wasn't Harlan, but this was one of Harlan's known associates.

"You're under arrest for breaking and entering. You have the right to remain silent—"

He snarled out another curse. "I'll say whatever I want."

Ignoring the asshole, Lincoln continued reading his rights as he hauled him out the door.

"No one else is with them," Deputy Lopez said as he approached the cabin. "They were the only two that arrived."

Lincoln inwardly cursed but kept his expression neutral. "Did your friend Harlan send you in here like some sacrificial lambs? Tell me where he is and we'll cut a deal. We don't care about you guys."

"He told us that—"

"Shut the hell up!" the man Lincoln had put in cuffs snapped at his partner. "You don't have anything on us. We're calling a lawyer as soon as we get to the station."

"But we didn't do anything—"

The man snarled again, cutting his friend off.

Lincoln had a feeling that as soon as they separated these two, he'd get the answers he wanted.

Unfortunately, any element of surprise they'd had was now gone. Clearly Harlan had realized this was a trap.

Or he'd at least been suspicious so he'd sent these guys in first. Either way, if Lincoln could get one of them to open up, it might give them a lead on where Harlan was hiding out.

CHAPTER THIRTY

Mac knocked on Adeline's bedroom door. Both his brothers were out in the living room, having ganged up on him and deciding to take over the night shift. He was exhausted, and considering that he and Adeline had spread it around town that they would be out at the Crescent Lake cabins tonight, he wasn't worried too much about Harlan finding them here. And one of Lincoln's guys was running patrol.

"Hey," she said as she opened the door.

She had on a tight T-shirt with sparkly purple hearts on the front and matching pajama pants. God she was gorgeous. Her shirt pulled taut over her chest and she definitely wasn't wearing a bra—something he was trying not to notice. "I'm probably going to crash soon. Joe and Dylan are keeping the night watch. Just wanted to let you know." He paused, his feet rooted to the floor in the hallway even though he wanted nothing more than to pick her up, lock the bedroom door behind them, then bury his face between her legs. But she hadn't let on that she wanted anything more and she was difficult to read.

Today, when they'd been acting like a real couple, he'd known deep down that was what he wanted. To be a couple with her. He wanted the whole damn town knowing she was his, *off-limits.*

239

And it should terrify him. He hadn't been with anyone in forever, had been so focused on his brothers and making sure they were raised with all the love and guidance they needed, that everything else had fallen by the wayside. But she made him feel alive, wanted. And he genuinely liked her—more than liked her. After being stuck under the same roof with her more than once, yeah, his feelings had solidified.

"I'll probably get some sleep too. Today was long." The smile she gave him was strained and he'd noticed at dinner that she'd been quiet.

"Is everything okay?"

She paused and for a moment he thought she was going to open up, but then she nodded. "Fine."

He narrowed his gaze slightly. That "fine" sounded anything but. "I want to kiss you right now," he blurted, even though that had been the last thing he'd been planning to say. *Real smooth, dumbass*, he chastised himself.

All the tension left her shoulders as she stared at him, her eyes widening in surprise. "What?"

"I'm not trying to pressure you or anything." He scrubbed a hand over his face. Dammit, he was screwing this up. They were stuck here for the foreseeable future—something that was just fine by him even though he hated the circumstances that had led here—and he didn't want things to be awkward. Didn't want to put unnecessary pressure on her. "I just...wanted to let you know. And now I sound like an asshole," he muttered. God, he really didn't have any game anymore.

She grabbed his hand and tugged him into the bedroom, shutting the door behind them with a soft snick. Her dark eyes were a mix of emotions as she looked up at him. "You want to kiss me? Real, and not pretend?"

"I wasn't pretending today." His gaze dropped to her full lips and his dick was instantly hard. Good God, this woman got right to the heart of him. She was in his blood at this point. His marrow. He wasn't sure how it had happened. They'd fallen into a sort of friendship out at the lake. And the bonus of that was that he craved her. More than his next breath. Maybe it was a bonus and a curse, because it was hard to think straight around her.

Without taking her gaze off his, she reached behind him and locked the door.

Damn, that was hot. But he didn't want to get ahead of himself. "Adeline..."

She stepped forward. "I promise I don't need words right now. Just you."

And that was exactly what he needed to hear.

Even though he wanted to pounce—he'd wanted her since the moment he'd laid eyes on her—he moved slowly, gently cupping her cheek as he lowered his head to hers. Emotions were high and he didn't want her to have any regrets. Ever.

But she had other ideas and grabbed onto his shoulders before jumping up and wrapping herself around him.

Okay, screw control. The energy sparking between them was palpable, a wild pulse in the air. But they had to be quiet. He'd never brought a woman home, and even though this wasn't his actual home he still didn't want his brothers to overhear them.

Her moans would be for him only.

He teased his tongue against hers as he clutched the back of her head with one hand and her ass with the other. God, she had the most perfect ass in the world.

He was aware of moving toward the bed as she writhed against him, her body rubbing up against him like a cat in heat.

Holy hell that was hot. Everything she did was hot.

He leaned back slightly as they reached the bed and grasped at her pajama top. "This is okay?" he murmured as he gripped the hem.

She nodded, and as soon as he'd pulled it over her head he sucked in a breath. Back at the lake house he'd avoided looking at her too much when he'd been undressing her, not wanting to take advantage when she'd been chilled to the bone.

Now she was showing herself to him. And his fantasy didn't compare to reality. Braless, stunning, her light brown nipples were tight little points...and he realized he was just staring like a fool.

"You're gorgeous," he rasped out, his entire body vibrating with a pent-up need that only she could ease. He felt almost disconnected from his body, as if this wasn't real and he was going to wake up and find out it was a dream.

Well, if it was a dream, he was going to jump in feetfirst while it lasted.

"You're pretty hot yourself, like a sexy lumberjack." Heat laced her words and she reached for the hem of his T-shirt, grabbing at it like a woman possessed.

He loved that she was as turned on for him as he was for her.

"For the record, it's been a while," she said. "So I hope I remember what I'm doing."

He let out a surprised burst of laughter. She was quite literally the most gorgeous woman he'd ever met so it was hard to imagine that she wasn't out there dating all the time. Some ridiculously primal part of him was glad though. "For the record, it's been a while for me too." Too damn long. And in that moment, he couldn't even remember anyone else. Because she was all that existed for him.

She was everything.

Her light brown skin seemed to glow softly in the muted light from the small lamp beside the bed, her curls wild and bouncing around her as he shifted them onto the sheets. And deep down he knew that one day he was going to put a ring on this woman's finger, if she would have him.

"I want to get you naked," she practically growled as she reached for the buckle of his jeans.

His cock jerked up against his pants at her hungrily spoken words, the wild heat of them.

But he knew that if he was naked he would lose control, so he needed to retain some of it.

Hell, just for a little longer. He needed to get her naked and he needed to get her off. He wanted her coming against his fingers or mouth. Both. Either. It didn't matter. But she needed to climax. Some primal part of him wanted her to know that he could and would take care of her. That she came first.

Grasping her hands, he drew them back from his body as he pinned her beneath him. "I want to taste between your legs first," he growled against her mouth. Because if she was touching him, he wasn't going to be able to focus.

In response, she arched her full breasts against his chest, the skin-to-skin sensation almost too much, almost sending him into sensory overload.

He slid his hands down her slim waist to her hips, savoring the feel of her soft skin underneath his palms as he pushed at her pajama pants.

She bit his bottom lip and somehow he managed to pull away, only to dip his head back down to one of her tightly budded nipples.

He sucked one into his mouth and immediately she gasped, arching for more. This woman was going to kill him, but what a way to go.

As he teased her, taking his time, she finished kicking her pants off. Next, he grasped the edge of her underwear and slowly eased them down her legs.

By the time he reached between her thighs, his cock throbbed painfully against his pants. He found her slick and open for him.

Hot damn. His cock reacted again, hard and pulsing, desperate to be freed, but it was too damn bad for him.

He'd waited an eternity for her, he could wait a little longer.

He slid two fingers inside her as he continued teasing her breasts and she rolled her hips against him, digging her fingers into his shoulders.

"Mac," she groaned quietly, probably as conscious as he was that they weren't alone in the house.

At this point he was finding it hard to care. Everything else funneled out around him. He just wanted her to climax, felt desperate with the need for it.

He switched to her other breast, letting her nipple go with a pop that seemed overly loud in the room. Briefly he wondered if his beard was abrading her soft skin, but from her moans, he didn't think so.

Then he worked his way down her body, kissing her everywhere, fascinated by her smooth skin.

He knew she had scars on her back, had seen them months ago out on the lake the day they'd found his brother. He wanted to kill the man who had put those on her, but he knew better than to ask for more details. She'd already told him a little about her past. He just hoped she trusted him enough to tell him everything one day. Adeline didn't need saving, but he would still slay dragons for her if she asked.

Her legs fell open as he finally reached her mound. He looked up the length of her lean body, found her watching him with unbridled hunger.

Her dark eyes were dilated, her breathing uneven. "I feel like I could come right now," she whispered as if it was a confession.

Oh hell yeah. He was on the brink of that too.

He slid his fingers deep inside her then dove between her legs, flicking his tongue against her clit. She was so slick and ready.

She let out a yelp that she quickly muffled but he didn't stop. She was on the edge and he was going to push her over.

He withdrew his fingers, then slooooooowly thrust them back inside. Her inner walls tightened around him with each push.

Over and over, he continued thrusting inside her as he teased her clit, not letting up on the pressure.

The more he teased, the more she jerked against his face. She liked what he was doing, a lot. And he loved that she was so responsive, that he didn't have to guess what turned her on.

She slid her fingers into his hair, clutched onto his head hard. "I'm so close," she said on a ragged whisper.

So he kept going, feeling drunk on her. He'd never been so desperate to make someone come, not even himself.

But this was a mountain he had to climb, had to conquer. He had to give her pleasure, give her everything she deserved.

Just like that, her inner walls started tightening around his fingers even harder and he knew she was close.

He sucked on her clit, exerting more pressure than before, and it set her off.

Her hips jerked upward and he felt the wave of her orgasm hit as she clenched tight around his fingers.

He wondered what it would feel like when she gripped his cock even as her climax rolled through her in sharp waves.

As she fell back against the bed, slowly coming down from her high, he managed to sit up and shove his own pants off. The fabric was painful against his cock, but then he was free.

He quickly retrieved a condom and somehow managed to roll it on.

She shoved up on her elbows, watching him with hungry, heated eyes as he loomed over her.

He laid the tip of his erection right over her no doubt still sensitive clit. It pulsed once, stroking against her.

"That was incredible," she murmured, gently raking her fingernails down his chest, over his abs and then wrapping those long, talented fingers around the base of his cock. She kept her gaze on him the whole time and he found himself hypnotized by her, unable to look away even if he'd wanted to.

She rolled her hips upward, guided him to her slick opening. He didn't need the help, but he loved the way she was putting him inside her. The way she was keeping her gaze pinned to his the whole time made it feel more intimate somehow, made him feel so incredibly connected to her.

She sucked in a breath as he pushed slowly inside her.

As he did, she looked almost surprised, her head falling back, her curls bouncing wildly as she arched her breasts upward.

She was a pure goddess in that moment, stretched out underneath him, sated from an orgasm, and he hoped to give her another one. Hell, another two or three.

He gritted his teeth as he pushed all the way to the hilt.

She was so damn tight and so damn wet and it was all for him.

She wrapped her arms and legs around him and he started thrusting, that drunk feeling back. Time didn't seem to have any meaning as he lost himself inside her.

Needing more connection, he crushed his mouth to hers, her tongue teasing against his, nipping back just as teasingly.

Even though all of this was fresh and new, it was like they'd been doing this forever.

He had no idea how she'd gotten so deep under his skin, but there she was. And there was no turning back now.

She slid her hands down his back, clutching onto his ass tight as she met him in another hard stroke.

He didn't know if it was possible for her, but he wanted to try to get her off again. So he reached between their bodies and slowed his strokes a fraction as he rubbed his thumb over her clit.

In that moment he felt a little ripple of her inner walls around his erection.

Oh damn, maybe she could.

Lazily, he began teasing her clit, rolling over the sensitive button in tight little circles.

He might as well have set off a firecracker because she jerked against him with a cry of pleasure and surprise.

That was when he knew she could climax again.

So he stayed where he was, on top of her and buried to the hilt as he continued teasing her clit.

Suddenly she dug her fingers into his ass. "Move," she demanded, the word a desperate plea.

He gave her exactly what she wanted and began thrusting. As he did, he felt the buildup of her orgasm.

Her inner walls felt amazing, clenching around him with each long stroke.

"Mac," she groaned, her body going bowstring tight right before she found another release.

His balls pulled up, his own release right on the brink. So he let go, giving in to the desperate hunger, his orgasm breaking free.

He cried out her name, unable to be as quiet as he wanted. Trying to muffle himself, he buried his face in her neck as she dug her fingers into his back, groaning against her hot skin.

Once again time had no meaning as they both came down from their high. Breathing hard, he simply held her for a long moment.

And though he hated to do it, he eventually eased out of her and disposed of the condom.

Then, moving as fast as possible, he hurried back to her. He didn't like being separated from her for even a moment.

She hadn't moved, the covers still tangled at the end of the bed, and she had one hand lazily stretched above her head. She really was a goddess, her long, lithe body a work of art.

And he would remember the sight of her like this for the rest of his life.

"You are amazing." He slid in next to her and she reached for him, curling her body right up against him, fitting perfectly.

"*You* are incredible." Yawning, she plastered herself to him.

In that moment he decided that talking could definitely wait. What else was there to say anyway? He grabbed the covers and pulled them over both of them, allowing sleep to take over. They both deserved some rest.

CHAPTER THIRTY-ONE

Adeline's eyes opened at a blaring sound. She jerked upward, her heart racing. Mac popped up next to her in a quick, fluid movement, looking wide-awake.

She blinked, trying to clear the haze from her mind. Rolling over, she saw that it was three in the morning. And that noise was getting more obnoxious. What was that... A car alarm. Then another one went off, and another.

"Stay here," he whispered, easing out of bed and sliding his pants on. He also pulled a pistol from out of the nightstand.

That was...jarring. But she stared at his tight ass for a moment, reality settling in as another alarm set off. Closer. Then he was out the door, moving like a ghost.

Feeling out of sorts, she mentally shook the cobwebs out of her head as she grabbed her underwear and pajamas from the floor, tugging them on. Tender between her legs, she moved toward the door but froze at a male voice from the front of the house.

"Put the gun down or I shoot your brother."

Oh my God. That had to be Harlan. Ice punched through her, destroying all the cobwebs. Someone was ordering Mac to drop his gun from the front of the house.

Panic wanted to set in but she refused to let it. Terror for Mac and his brothers exploded inside her, but she knew she only had moments to react if they wanted to get out of this alive. To get help for them. She grabbed her phone, moved to the bedroom window and slid it open.

She'd started dialing Lincoln even as she lifted her leg over the windowsill. She'd contemplated 911 but figured Lincoln would respond faster and would ask fewer questions.

She didn't have a weapon and knew that Hayward would use her against Mac and his brothers. No way in hell was she going to let that happen.

"Adeline, is everything okay?" Lincoln's voice was tired but he sounded awake enough.

"Harlan's got Mac at gunpoint," she whispered as she hurried to the front of the house. As she did, she saw a big decorative rock in the shape of flip-flops propped up along the front landscaping. She picked it up and nearly dropped it, not expecting it to be so heavy. "I climbed out a bedroom window and called you. I don't know if his brothers are okay." Oh God, she hoped so.

"Where's Mac in the house?"

Carefully she peered around to the front patio. Multiple car alarms were going off in the neighborhood, lights flashing in various driveways. Maybe he'd used that as a distraction to break in? She didn't know. The place didn't have an alarm system because it was a new rental, but Joe and Dylan were supposed to have been keeping watch.

"I heard someone in the living room ordering Mac to put his gun down or the intruder would shoot his brother. I snuck out the window and called you." Her heart was an erratic, wild thing out of control in her chest, but she forced herself to remain calm. "It's got to be Harlan and I don't know if he's alone."

"Run and hide somewhere. Get to safety. I'm on the way and so is backup." He sounded fully awake now, muffled sounds in the background.

"Keep your sirens off." She was worried Harlan would shoot Mac dead if he heard the cops coming.

"Of course. Get somewhere safe *now*," he ordered. "Mac is smart and highly trained, so don't get caught and used as a hostage."

"Okay." She hung up, and while she wanted to do as he'd said...she was terrified it would be too late by the time law enforcement got here. Right now she needed to create a distraction that allowed Mac to get away or take Hayward down. She refused to abandon Mac and his brothers.

She ran into the front yard, hauled the painted rock back and threw it with all her might at the nearest living room window.

As the glass shattered, a gunshot went off, stopping her heart. *Mac!*

* * *

Mac slowly set his weapon on the living room floor. But he didn't take his eyes off Harlan the entire time.

Inwardly cursing himself, he swept the scene. Joe was on the ground, his head bleeding, and hopefully just knocked out. Not... *No*, Mac refused to consider the other possibility.

Dylan was in front of Harlan, his hands up, his expression livid.

"Call your girlfriend out here too," Harlan ordered, the look on his face dark. Set. He had on dark jeans, gloves, a navy hoodie and a matching cap pulled low.

Mac didn't raise his hands, just stared at Harlan. "This is between me and you. Let them go."

Harlan laughed, the sound maniacal as he peered slightly around Dylan's big frame. Oh, he knew what he was doing, using Dylan as cover. *Damn it, damn it, damn it!*

Mac couldn't make a move yet, couldn't put either of his brothers in danger. But no way in hell was he calling for Adeline. He just hoped she'd gotten out of the house and called 911.

"You think I'm stupid? I'm not letting them go. I'm going to kill both of them and make you watch. But first...Adeline!" Harlan called out, his eyes wide, dilated.

Stay in the bedroom, Mac mentally ordered her. *Or climb out the damn window. Anything, just don't come out here. No, no, no.*

"Walk out here or I put a bullet in your boyfriend," he called out, his voice rising with each word.

"How did you find us?" Mac needed to keep this lunatic talking. He had to buy time, long enough for Adeline to call Lincoln. He might not get out of this alive, but he was going to make sure Adeline and his brothers did.

"It's a small town." Again, there was just a hint of mania in his tone.

Ice slid down Mac's spine. Verona Bay was a small town, but Harlan finding them here was disturbing. And he hadn't actually answered. "You're never going to get away with this."

He snorted, his eyes flaring wide. "I've killed before and I'll kill again, asshole. I'm going to kill *you* tonight and enjoy every second."

"Look, you can still let my brothers walk away." Mac knew it was useless at this point, but he hoped his talking had at least bought Adeline enough time to escape. He forced himself to focus on that and not his brothers. He hated that they were in this mess.

"Enough talk." Harlan glanced over his shoulder toward the front door, as if looking for someone.

He had to know that time was ticking, that Adeline would have called for help by now.

Mac took two subtle steps forward, closing the distance between them as quickly as he could. He didn't stare directly at Harlan's weapon hand, but it was in his periphery. His objectives were simple—disarm Harlan, keep his family safe.

Harlan looked at his watch and stamped his foot once like a toddler, spit flying out of his mouth as he snarled. "It looks like I'm not going to have any fun with your girl! And I'm sure the cops are on the way by now."

Then he straightened, aiming his pistol directly at Dylan's head. "Say goodbye to your—"

A crack rent the air.

Glass shattered and Harlan jumped, spinning around. As he did, Dylan elbowed him in the ribs, knocking him off-balance.

Mac was already in motion, diving over the couch before he tackled Harlan right into a wall. Plaster cracked under their combined weight. The gun went off, firing into the ceiling above their heads.

Mac scrambled to get control of it, slamming a fist into Harlan's face. As he did, the pistol fell to the floor.

On a cry of rage, Harlan drove his fist into Mac's ribs.

He barely felt it as he hauled back and decked Harlan square in the jaw, sending him reeling backward into the busted wall.

Harlan slumped to the floor, his head slamming against a side table as he went down in a crumpled heap.

"Grab restraints!" Mac snapped to Dylan, who'd already moved into action, doing just that. With a belt in hand, he was securing Harlan's wrists as Mac knelt down next to Joe and called out for Adeline. "Adeline!"

"Joe, open your eyes," Dylan said.

To Mac's surprise and relief, Joe groaned softly as Mac rolled him over, his eyes blinking open slowly. "Bastard hit me," he growled, reaching up to touch the side of his head.

It was a shallow gash, thank God.

The fifty-ton weight on his chest lifted. "Don't talk. Just sit still while I grab some ice." He popped up but bypassed the kitchen, needing to see Adeline first. As he stepped into the bedroom, he immediately saw that the window was open. Once again another wave of relief overcame him, nearly bowling him over. She must have escaped out the window, had likely thrown that rock through it. Her phone was gone too. She'd done just what he'd hoped. He grabbed his own phone anyway, ready to call 911 regardless.

"Mac?" Dylan called out as he heard the front door open. There was something in his brother's tone that set off alarm bells.

Going on instinct, Mac dove out the window as well. Someone had set off those car alarms, so it stood to reason that Harlan had a partner.

He shoved up from the grass and hurried along the side of the house. Adrenaline ripped through him, his earlier relief at Adeline having escaped morphing into something else. If Harlan's partner had gotten to her... Mac peered around the corner and stilled. Chief of Police Robert Hayward had a weapon trained on Adeline as he shoved her through the front door.

Rage swelled inside him as he quickly weighed his options.

Going on instinct and a desperate need to protect his family, he hoisted himself up onto the patio and quietly hurried across the planks. He would have to move fast, strike now instead of waiting for law enforcement.

If they got involved in a standoff, shit would surely end badly.

As he neared the closing front door, he kicked it open with his boot, slamming it into the chief.

But Hayward was more trained than his pathetic son. The man stumbled back, still holding his pistol as Mac attacked.

He grabbed Hayward's wrist as the man lashed out with a fist, jabbing him in the ribs.

A sense of savagery overtook him as he leaned into it. Let the guy pummel him. He had to get him down and keep him down. Had to stop him from hurting his brothers and Adeline.

Hayward jabbed him in the ribs again. Mac sucked in a breath as pain shot through his side, but he held on to the man's wrist, clamping down, and slammed it against the floor until Hayward released the weapon.

Hayward cursed and threw a wild punch at his face, but Mac dodged it and rolled slightly, keeping him pinned as he slammed his elbow into Hayward's face.

"I'm going to kill you," the man snarled.

"Stop right now!" Adeline screamed.

They both froze and he looked up to find her training the pistol right on Robert Hayward, her arms completely steady, her expression ice-cold.

"You're not gonna do anything," the man snarled with derision. "Bet you don't even know how to use a gun, so why don't you put it down and—"

She shifted the weapon slightly to the left and pulled the trigger.

The floor next to them exploded, wood flying up everywhere.

Hayward froze, remaining where he was on the floor.

Shocked at Adeline's aim, Mac moved quickly, rolling him over and slamming his face against the floor. And he wasn't gentle about it. He yanked the man's arms behind his back, vaguely aware of lights flashing through the front windows.

Suddenly Lincoln was racing through the door.

He took in the scene, cursed and pulled out his cuffs. He quickly snapped some on the chief just as Harlan started stirring.

Mac jumped to his feet and rushed toward Adeline, who'd already put the weapon down. Immediately he pulled her to his chest.

Dylan was crouched next to Joe who was sprawled on the couch, looking green. "Joe needs an ambulance now. He was hit in the head and I don't know how hard."

Lincoln nodded and shouted orders to deputies who poured into the house, taking over immediately.

As two EMTs hurried in, Mac said, "I know we have to make statements, but I'm going to the hospital with my brother, and Adeline and Dylan are coming with me. Harlan broke in and was going to kill us. Then his father showed up. We're not going anywhere except the hospital, so just find us there."

It was clear that Lincoln wanted to argue, but he nodded and frog-marched Robert Hayward out the front door. Hayward simply looked at the ground as he was hauled out.

"You okay to drive?" Adeline asked.

He nodded, leaning down and brushing his lips over hers. "I'm just so glad you're okay. That was a pretty amazing shot. I had no idea you knew how to use a pistol."

"I have a lot of secrets," she whispered, and there was something in her eyes he couldn't define.

He didn't care what her secrets were though, as long as he got to spend the rest of his life getting to know all of them. For now, however, he was just damn glad she and his brothers were alive.

CHAPTER THIRTY-TWO

"Pretty sure he just keeps getting hurt because he likes to flirt with the staff here," Dylan said as he snagged the Jell-O from Joe's hospital tray.

"Hey!" Joe made a half-assed grab for it.

Adeline smiled at their antics, even though she was still reeling from everything, still trying to process it. Right now she figured that a week of sleep and a real vacation—with Mac—might help.

"You don't eat green anyway." Dylan dug his spoon into it.

"I talked to Marcy, and she's on her way home." Mac stepped back into the room and immediately moved to Adeline's side.

"You didn't have to call her." But Joe looked happy that she was coming home.

Adeline snorted softly. "He didn't, technically. She'd called your phone a few times and he finally answered."

"I'm more embarrassed than anything. I wish they would just discharge me. I don't need to be here." Joe crossed his arms over his chest, making him look even younger than his nineteen years.

"You previously had a head injury and know more than most how dangerous they can be." Mac's tone was hard. "So no arguments. You stay here as long as the doctors require it."

Joe mock saluted. "Yes, sir," he said with more than a touch of sarcasm.

"Can we get you anything?" Adeline asked. "Other than busting you out of here? Maybe we can grab you something from the house?"

"Yeah, my tablet would be good. And..." He rattled off a list with precision.

"Dude, you're staying for like one more day." Dylan finally cut him off.

"Oh, I also want my weighted blanket," Joe continued, ignoring his brother.

Which started a weird conversation about how Joe had stolen Dylan's blanket and how Dylan wouldn't be giving it up for him, even though he was in the hospital.

"Are they always like this?" Adeline murmured to Mac as they stepped back from the two.

"All the time. Usually worse." He scrubbed a hand over his face, looking as exhausted as she felt. "They're like five-year-olds and have only been putting on a show of relative maturity for you. Apparently they're letting you see the real them now."

"We can *hear* you," Joe grumbled.

At a soft knock on the door, they turned to find Lincoln stepping inside in uniform, looking very official.

When his gaze landed on Joe, the tension in his expression eased. "They told me you were okay, but I'm glad to see it. How are you feeling?"

"I'm great," Joe said with a nonchalant shrug, as if he hadn't been attacked and knocked out. "Ready to get discharged."

"So what's the deal?" Mac asked, a hint of impatience in his tone.

Adeline understood. They'd already made official statements about the whole ordeal, but they wanted answers, wanted to know for sure that Harlan and his father would be paying for their crimes.

"Both men have been arrested and charged, officially. I might not like the guy, but I don't think the chief was behind any of the murders, or even involved in them. However, he figured out where you guys were staying through illegal means. At least from what we've gathered so far. And I guess he'd been keeping an eye on your place and saw when Harlan broke in. But instead of stopping him...he held you at gunpoint," he said pointedly to Adeline. "I don't know what he intended to do, honestly. I don't know if he did either. But the soon-to-be former chief is under arrest and officially under investigation for crimes not related to his son's." Lincoln rolled his eyes. "There's a lot of stuff we're unpacking right now, but the DA has officially charged them, and the list of charges will likely grow as our investigation uncovers more information."

"So did he just set off all the car alarms as a distraction?" Adeline asked. Dylan had told them that he'd heard something on the front porch after the first car alarm had gone off. He'd opened the door to see what was going on and Harlan had jumped him, taken him down from the side. When Joe had tried to intervene, Harlan had slammed his pistol against his head and knocked him out. Dylan was still beating himself up over it.

"His girlfriend did. She's under arrest as an accessory. We...don't know if she's involved in the murders either. Everything's a mess but we're getting it all untangled. I just wanted to stop by again and make sure you were okay, Joe."

"Thanks, sheriff. I'm good." And he really did seem like he was.

"If you need anything from us, just call me," Mac said. "We're probably going to clear out soon when the nurses kick us out."

There was another knock on the door before Lincoln could answer. To Adeline's surprise, Serenity and her daughter Harper hurried inside.

"What are you guys doing here?"

"We brought you a little bag of goodies," Serenity said as Harper raced at Adeline and jumped into her arms.

Adeline scooped the little girl up and held her close. She smelled like sugar cookies and sunshine. "Ooh, I've missed you, sweet girl."

Harper giggled and jumped down, placed her hands on her hips. "I've missed you too. Guess what?" She grinned to reveal that she was missing a tooth.

"Wow! Is the tooth fairy bringing you anything?"

"Aunt Adeline! The tooth fairy isn't real," she said admonishingly, as if Adeline didn't know anything. "Not like Santa."

"Ah, my mistake. I was clearly misinformed."

"It's okay. I make mistakes all the time. So mommy says you have a boyfriend now." Harper stared up at her with big blue eyes the same color as Serenity's.

"Ah…" Boyfriend? Were they a couple now? Her brain short-circuited and she couldn't even look at Mac. They had way too much of an audience right now.

Serenity moved in closer, giving Adeline an apologetic smile as she hugged her. "I'm so glad you're okay," Serenity murmured, before turning to Harper. "We'll talk about that later."

Before Harper could respond, Lucas stepped into the room, smiling at Mac and greeting him in that way that guys did with the hug and fist bump. Mac had been a steady rock over the last few hours, keeping her mind calm at the hospital when she'd finally come down from her adrenaline high. She'd slept on his shoulder for a while, and when she'd woken up he'd been there, calm and steady.

"You guys were supposed to stay in the waiting room," Lincoln said, frowning at his brother.

"Yeah, well, Mia Jackson is working this shift and she loves Adeline and me, so she let us come back here. So deal with it." Serenity lifted a dark eyebrow, daring her brother-in-law to say anything.

"Yeah, Uncle Lincoln, deal with it," Harper mimicked, then cackled maniacally before she raced over to stand directly next to the IV and started asking Joe questions about it and his "hurt head" and how he felt.

"Autumn's here too," Lucas murmured. "She'll probably be in here in a second. She was talking to someone she knew though. And...I got a text from Easton saying he wanted to stop by and check on everyone."

Lincoln scrubbed a hand over his face and muttered something about no one in his family listening to him. Then he shook his head and looked over at Mac and Adeline. "I'm going to get out of here, then. I'll be in touch with you guys in a couple hours. Your rental is a crime scene for now, but you're fine to go home."

As he left, Serenity pulled Adeline into another big hug. "I can't believe what happened. I know I've said it, but I'm so glad you're okay. Do you want to come stay with us for a while? If you don't want to be by yourself, we'd love to have you."

Mac wrapped his arm around Adeline's shoulders and kissed the top of her head as he pulled her close. "She's staying with me."

Ooooh. There was a note of possessiveness in his voice she felt all the way to her core. Now wasn't the time for that, but her body still reacted to that hot, protective tone.

Serenity nodded and continued. "What do you guys need? More food? We've got some frozen meals I can bring over."

"Honestly nothing." Mac answered before Adeline could and she was grateful, because her brain was fried and she simply wanted to sit down. "Joe's going to be discharged this afternoon, so we're just going to head home and crash for a while."

"Hey," Joe called out. "You told me it would be tomorrow."

"I lied. Now stop complaining." Mac didn't turn around as he answered. He'd told Joe tomorrow in case the doctor changed his mind.

"What about at the house? I heard it got shot up a little bit," Lucas said as Harper hung on to one of his arms, walking around him in circles and counting each "lap."

"It's going to take some repairs. The wall, a window, part of the floor. But everyone's alive and relatively unharmed. I'm more than fine with repairs." Mac squeezed her once and she leaned into him.

"Just tell me what you need. I can get a crew down there and we can fix everything up as soon as the scene is released," Lucas said.

"Thanks man, I appreciate it."

Adeline knew that they worked together occasionally, with Lucas hiring him for specific custom pieces that customers requested.

They talked for a little while until Joe said he was tired and crashed less than sixty seconds later, exhaustion taking him under.

After that, Adeline and Mac left too. She needed some of her things if she was going to stay at his place, and by the time they'd made it back to her house, she was surprised she was still awake. "You think we could crash for a couple hours here?" she asked him. "I mean, if you want to."

"Hell yeah. Dylan said he wanted to head home and take care of a few things. But he doesn't need us for anything right now. And Joe's fine."

Those words were music to her ears.

Stepping into her house, she breathed in the familiar scents. She'd missed her place, her safe haven. It was kind of weird having Mac in her space, but she liked it. Her things were delicate, feminine, a little eccentric, and he was this big, burly lumberjack. But she thought he looked perfect in her kitchen. And she *knew* he would look perfect in her bedroom.

"I know we haven't officially talked," he started, his body growing tense as he leaned against her center island.

She tensed too, leaning against one of the countertops across from him. "Talk?"

"About this thing between us." He motioned between their bodies, his blue eyes intense. "I want things official. I don't want to date anyone else, and I sure as hell don't want you dating anyone else. I'm too punchy right now to be...eloquent, I guess. So I'm laying it all out there, Adeline Rodriguez. I want to be with you. Just you and me. Together."

She was feeling punchy too, but his words set off something inside her. She jumped at him, practically attacking as she wrapped her legs around him. She'd sworn to herself that she'd never let her guard down around anyone again. Not a man, anyway. And she'd believed that lie. Thankfully she was smart enough to see the folly of her vow, because Mac wasn't just anyone.

He was everything.

"It's just you and me. Officially," she murmured, right before he kissed her.

CHAPTER THIRTY-THREE

Christmas Day

"And this is for you," Joe said, handing Adeline the last box that had been lingering under the red-and-gold decorated Christmas tree.

Mac and his brothers had asked her to spend Christmas Day with them, though she'd actually spent Christmas Eve here too—in Mac's bed. She'd been here practically every night for the last week.

It was weird being with people on Christmas morning. Normally she spent Christmas with friends, but that was always in the afternoon after she'd spent Christmas morning alone. This...was different. Way better. She liked being here with them, feeling like she was part of their little family. Though she didn't want to get too ahead of herself, even if her feelings for Mac were so big it was hard to put into words.

"This is too much," she said even as she tore into the gift. She gasped as she pulled out the delicately carved wooden box. She looked up at Mac, who was sitting across from her, coffee mug in hand and a grin on his face. God, he looked so sexy in his Santa pajama pants with his dark hair rumpled.

"You couldn't have had time to make this in the last week!" Not with how detailed it was.

His grin widened, and oh yeah, he was proud of himself. Well, he should be. "I've been working on it for you for a while."

Tears threatened to sting her eyes, but she quickly blinked them away. "Really?"

"Yeah, I was...hopeful where you were concerned."

Oh God, this man. "It's beautiful, thank you." She traced her fingers over the top, savoring the intricately carved shapes of paintbrushes, a sewing machine and other symbols of art and things that represented her.

"Look inside," Dylan said as he stepped back into the room, his own coffee mug in hand.

She popped it open and found...a T-shirt? She pulled it out and started laughing when she read the front: *I'm so tired of winning.* She snickered and tugged it on over her pajama top even as she nodded at Joe, who pulled out the gift she'd hidden behind one of the couches.

"What's this?" Mac asked as Joe set it in front of him.

"You're not the only one who likes to make gifts." She grinned and picked up her forgotten mug, took a sip of the hazelnut-infused coffee. "Open it," she demanded when he kept looking at the bag.

Grinning in that panty-melting way of his, he pulled the tissue paper stuffing out, then withdrew the quilt she'd made for him.

She'd started making it with him in mind, but hadn't been sure if she could finish in time for Christmas. Luckily she'd had enough time the last couple days to complete it. She'd created sixteen pinwheel blocks using custom fabric and contrasted the darker fabric with white sashing and a white border. The result was a quilt that looked a lot more intricate and time-consuming than it actually was.

Standing, he unfolded it and stared at it with a touch of awe. "This is gorgeous."

"I remember you said something about getting more in touch with your Scottish heritage, so I found some specialty fabric on Etsy for the pinwheels."

"You must have busted your ass to finish this." Sitting back down, he looked over at her with all sorts of heat in his blue eyes.

"I did." An answering heat coiled in her belly as he continued watching her.

Right about now she wished it was just the two of them, because the look in his eyes promised a whole lot of pleasure.

"I have an announcement to make," Dylan said abruptly, dispersing the hot tension between her and Mac.

For now. She turned to look at Dylan as he stood.

Dylan wiped his palms on his pajama pants, all his focus on Mac as he spoke. "I'm joining the Marines when I'm done with school. As an officer."

The room went silent as Mac stared at his brother for a long moment. Then he stood, stepped forward and pulled him into a big hug, which was clearly the right thing to do because all the tension in Dylan's shoulders eased. Joe moved in too, tackling both of them.

"That's great news." Adeline jumped to her own feet and joined the others, giving Dylan a big hug.

He seemed so young to her but she knew he was definitely old enough to make the choice. And after everything that had gone down before, he was handling things like a champ. So he was mature enough too.

Mac had told her last night that Dylan seemed like he had something on his mind lately, and Adeline was guessing this was it. He'd probably been waiting to tell his big brother.

"I have an announcement to make too," Joe said, clearing his throat almost nervously.

"You're not joining the military," Mac muttered. "Any branch."

Joe laughed lightly, shaking his head. "No. But Marcy and I have been talking, and we've decided to move in together."

Mac's eyes widened slightly but Adeline wasn't exactly surprised. It had been clear to her at least that Joe and Marcy had been heading toward this.

"Wow, well that's great." Mac looked more shell-shocked by this news than he had about Dylan's.

She wrapped her arm around Joe and squeezed him close. "It is great, Joe. You guys are sweet together."

He lifted a shoulder. "Figured it was time."

"Yeah," Dylan said to Mac. "You've been taking care of us forever. It's time you had some privacy of your own anyway."

Mac didn't respond, just pulled them into a hug, his biceps and forearms flexing as he wrapped them up in his big arms.

Deciding to give them privacy, Adeline stepped out of the living room and headed to the kitchen. She poured herself another mug of coffee, smiling as she listened to the faint Christmas music playing in the air. That was all Joe. He'd woken all of them up this morning like a kid. And when they'd come out, music had been playing and coffee had already been made.

Mac stepped into the kitchen a few moments later, making a beeline for her.

Taking her off guard, he scooped her up in his arms and hugged her tight. Burying her face against his neck, she inhaled his rich scent.

"A lot of changes are happening," he rumbled against her as he put her back down.

"Good ones, I think."

He nodded, his intense eyes pinning her in place. Oh, she recognized that look by now. They were about to go back to his room and get naked. "I need to say something. It's just...I love you," he blurted as he watched her.

She froze, her eyes widening.

"I know we've only been together a couple weeks. You don't have to say anything, but I know how I feel and—"

"I love you too!" She'd only been stunned for a second because she hadn't realized he was in the same place as her. But she'd been there for a while. She'd realized she loved him before today. "I'm not saying it just because you did. I've known since the night... Well, since the night of everything. I knew at the hospital for sure." Back when she'd thought she might lose him, everything had crystallized in her mind so damn clearly.

Even if things didn't work out in the end, she had no regrets with Mac sexy-as-hell Collins. She loved him so much. There were still parts of her past she wanted to tell him about, but not on Christmas Day. For now, she simply wanted to savor this new phase in their relationship. And hold on tight.

He grinned and lowered his mouth to hers, quickly deepening the kiss into something hot and heavy and—

Someone cleared their throat and she looked up to find both his brothers walking into the kitchen, smothering their smiles.

"Sorry, guys. Marcy's gonna be here soon and I'm starving. We need to make a proper Christmas breakfast." Joe headed to the fridge and started pulling out eggs. God, he really had grown up.

"I'm going to grab a shower, then." She eased back slightly, her body revved up and ready to go. But that was going to have to wait, unfortunately.

"We've got breakfast," Dylan said. Then he grinned at his brother. "Why don't you go grab a shower too?"

Mac simply grabbed her hand and tugged her out of the kitchen toward his bedroom.

The heat that had been simmering inside her expanded, taking over. "Merry Christmas to me," she murmured as he pinned her up against his closed bedroom door, already tugging at her pajamas.

This was by far the best way she'd ever spent Christmas.

CHAPTER THIRTY-FOUR

Adeline pushed up from her chair at Sweet Spot, smiling at her friends. They'd had an impromptu get-together after she and Serenity had gotten off work to talk about an upcoming festival for spring and how they were going to drive business to all the places downtown. But she knew Mac would be here soon to pick her up—her car was in the shop again—and she could admit she was ready to see him.

"Oh girl, I know that look." Autumn sat back in her chair, a grin on her face. "You're ready to see your man."

"Uh, yeah." She picked up her purse, hooked it over her shoulder. "Don't act like you're not ready to see yours." It was only February so Adeline and Mac were definitely still in their honeymoon phase and she loved every second of it. Two months officially together and she couldn't keep her hands off him.

"It's true. Ugh, I'm horny all the time now. I think I'm scaring Lincoln." Autumn stretched slightly, her baby bump even bigger than the last time Adeline had seen her a week ago. She rested her left hand on her stomach, the glint from her fairly new engagement ring sparkling under the lights.

Serenity snickered into her hot tea. "Yeah, somehow I don't believe that."

Bianca rounded from behind the countertop, a carafe of decaf in hand as she approached the table. "Make your escape now before she starts talking about different positions. I had to listen to her earlier talk about 'pregnancy positions.'"

"Hey, you asked!" Autumn threw a balled-up napkin at Bianca, who ducked to avoid it.

Bianca just snickered and continued pouring coffee.

"All right, children," Maris Carson, former elementary school teacher who now ran a shelter for abused women, lightly tapped on the table. She really had that teacher thing down pat. "Adeline, we'll see you later. The rest of you, we need to figure out how to keep the parking situation..."

Adeline quickly waved and hurried out, losing most of the conversation as she stepped out into the chilly air. She knew that in barely a month, however, it would be spring and everything would be blooming—and she was ready for some warmth and color everywhere. The town was decorated for Valentine's Day—all the shops downtown had windows full of red, white and pink, and the florist was making bank this month.

Mac was parked along the curb and started his Bronco, flashing his lights once as if she hadn't seen him pull up.

Laughing, she hurried down the sidewalk to meet him, but he was out and had opened her door before she'd made it.

"Missed you." He brushed his lips over hers, deepening it for only a moment before standing back to let her get into the passenger seat. Then he waited until she was seated and strapped in to shut it behind her.

He really was the best.

And she felt like she'd hit the jackpot. But she knew she needed to tell him the truth about her past—about all of it. "Can we talk tonight?" she asked as he shut his door behind him.

He stilled, his fingers on the wheel as he turned to look at her. "Are you breaking up with me?"

She snorted and reached out, squeezed his leg. "No way. But..." She swallowed hard past the lump in her throat. "You might see me differently after I tell you what I need to." He might break up with her, something she was trying to steel herself for. She trusted Mac's love, but her fear ran deep—and her secret was big.

"What is it?"

She glanced around, saw her friends still inside through the big front window. "Can we not do it here?"

"Of course." He placed his hand over hers, squeezed once in a comforting gesture much like she'd just done to him, and pulled away from the curb. "So how was tonight?"

"Fun, and productive. A good combo." She loved that he wasn't pushing her. "Did you get the chair finished?"

He grinned, a look of utter relief crossing his rugged features. "Yeah. And my delivery guy picked it up late for me so it's on the way to its new owner."

He'd been working on a gorgeous custom rocking chair for weeks and she'd enjoyed seeing the progress.

Even though she was sad to see it go. Thankfully his shop was back up and running, thanks to the construction crew he'd hired—one of Lucas's crews, of course—and he'd even taken on a mentee to train. "You know I'm going to ask for one soon, right?"

He laughed lightly. "And you should know I saw the way you were eyeing it and already started on one for you."

"I seriously love you." So much so. And it was the real kind, not the crap she'd thought was love when she was young and stupid and just looking for someone to love her back in a way she craved. This was the forever kind.

His soft smile was firmly in place as he pulled into her driveway, and the levity faded as she prepared to rip the Band-Aid off. He started to turn the Bronco off but she stopped him.

"Let's just do this out here."

"Are you sure?" Unstrapping, he turned to face her.

"Yeah." That way if he decided he didn't want to be with her anymore, he could just go and she could go bawl her eyes out inside. "I told you about my ex and my mom and…everything that happened."

He nodded, taking her hand in his as he listened.

"My ex came after me again. He…was going to kill me. He had a knife and spelled out explicitly what he was going to do to me." She closed her eyes for a moment, swallowed hard. She'd never told anyone about this, and getting it out was harder than she'd imagined. And she'd actually practiced in her head telling Mac all this.

"You don't have to do this now. You can tell me the rest later." Distress laced his voice as he squeezed her hand again.

"No." She watched him, felt more grounded by his steady presence. "I want to tell you all of this now and then never talk about it again. When he came for me, I was prepared. I must have known deep down that I'd never escape him, no matter how far I moved. By that point, I was living in Delray Beach in a little house I loved. I was working at an art gallery and..." She cleared her throat. "He broke into my house on the Fourth of July. I don't know if the date was intentional, if he wanted the fireworks to mute my screams but, in the end, it worked in my favor."

She took a deep breath, forcing herself to continue. "What I didn't tell you is that when he ran from the murder scene at my mom's house, he left his gun behind. Obviously I don't think it was intentional. I didn't find it until I was packing up, getting ready to put all her stuff in storage. It had fallen under one of her couches. I assumed he'd taken it with him and obviously the cops did too. But he must have lost it when I shoved him and ran. I'll never know why. I...kept it. And I started going to a gun range to get practice. I don't like guns—I hate them, in fact. But I knew he'd never let me go. That he'd kill me if he got the chance. When he broke in, we got into a scuffle and I shot him. Just once, and it was right in the middle of his chest. I thought someone would call the cops but the fireworks in my neighborhood had been so loud that night, and almost everyone but me was at the community pool watching them together."

"Jesus." Mac scooted closer, holding both her hands in his. "I'm so sorry, Adeline."

"I...never called the cops. I was in shock, terrified of so many things. But I was really scared of getting charged with murder. After my mom was murdered, they treated me like it was my fault for getting involved with him. Like I brought this on my mom. And..." Her voice cracked slightly. "Maybe it was my fault. After that, I had no faith in the system at all. And I wasn't going to take the chance that I'd be arrested and wrongfully convicted. And even if it was deemed self-defense—which it was—he had a lot of scary friends. I didn't know if they would come after me—I think at least two of them might have. So I made a split-second choice. A friend of mine had a boat he let me use on occasion so I drove out into the ocean and dumped his body the next night. It's one of the single most terrifying moments of my life."

She'd been so sure she would be caught on the drive, and then she'd thought she'd get caught at the little marina. But she never had. It was like nothing at all had changed in her life, when in reality everything had.

"I moved not long after that, wanting to put everything about him behind me." She'd also been sick over everything for months, living in fear of being caught.

"That's..."

"Too much to handle? Do you hate me?" God, he was probably disgusted by her.

"I'm so sorry you had to deal with all that alone. I'm sorry you had to make such a hard choice because you had no other *good* choices. And of course I don't hate you. I love you. Nothing will change that, Adeline. You're my person."

She shoved out a ragged sigh, tears escaping, falling down her cheeks before she could stop them.

He cupped her face, wiping them away as he kissed her, murmuring soft things she couldn't make out because of the sheer relief punching through her. Mac knew everything about her and he still loved her. Didn't judge her at all.

Looking back, she sometimes wondered if she'd made the right choice, but then she stopped questioning herself. She'd made the right choice for her situation and didn't have room for regrets. Not when everything had led her to this wonderful man.

"You're my person too," she murmured against his mouth, warmth spreading through her when he pulled her into his arms.

"You ready to get inside and out of the cold?" The heat in his eyes promised he would have no problem warming her up.

In that moment she knew she'd made the right choice in telling him all her secrets. If she hadn't, it would have weighed on her forever, eaten her up inside. And now she knew Mac loved her for exactly who she was. She would never have to wonder.

And she loved him right back. "Oh yeah."

EPILOGUE

Ten months later

Mac stared as Adeline started walking down the aisle to a song she'd chosen. Very nontraditional, just like her—and his breath caught in his throat, unable to look away from the woman he was about to marry. They'd decided to get married at a local place—an elegant rustic barn that had been renovated years ago with hardwood floors, brick columns in the interior. Now sheer drapes and what seemed like a million twinkle lights illuminated the place.

His brothers were his best men but she'd asked both of them to walk her down the aisle and they'd agreed. And they'd been surprisingly choked up about it. Or maybe not surprisingly—they loved her almost as much as he did. But in a very different way.

Her curls were wild and free with little flowers laced throughout, and her dress was formfitting up top but flowing the rest of the way to her ankles. Her movements were liquid grace as she glided toward him.

She looked like a fairy queen as she walked, and she *was* a queen. His Queen.

His eyes connected with hers and the force of the day hit him full center, right in the chest. A grin split his face and he couldn't stop smiling. He was about to marry the woman he loved, a woman who'd opened up his world, his heart, with her goodness and humor. She was better than anything he could have ever imagined for himself. She was a damn survivor and he was glad she was doing more than just surviving, but living. And he counted himself lucky that he got to walk beside her through life.

Everyone else around them funneled out as she continued walking. Then she was standing in front of him and he grasped her hands in his, needing to touch her. He was vaguely aware of his brothers stepping off to the side to take their places, vaguely aware of her bridesmaids on the other side of her.

Then Bianca—also her bridesmaid, who'd gotten a license just so she could marry them—started talking.

Thankfully she kept things short, and they both said their vows and then he *finally* got to kiss her. She hadn't stayed with him last night, and that one night had felt like an eternity without her in his bed. When they both finally came up for air she was breathless, her eyes sparkling, and the crowd around them laughed lightly.

Because maybe he'd gotten carried away just a little bit. But come on, he was marrying the sweetest, most beautiful woman in the world. How could he *not* get carried away?

"I love you," she murmured as they started back down the aisle.

"I love you too. Now and forever."

* * *

"Care if I cut in for a dance?" Joe asked as he sidled up to Mac and Adeline.

"Only if you promise to stop sneaking drinks," Adeline admonished as she pulled him in to dance.

"Better keep it short, little brother," Mac growled as he stepped back. He did not share well.

Adeline just grinned and pulled her new brother-in-law onto the dance floor. "You're not very sneaky and you're still underage." And given that alcoholism ran in his family, she hoped he stopped drinking altogether.

"I know," he groaned as he started dancing to the music. And the boy did not have any rhythm.

But he was adorable, and both he and Dylan had been wonderful as she and Mac had planned the wedding. But Joe's girlfriend was out of the country for a semester abroad for school and she knew he was feeling down. Still… "You know alcohol doesn't solve anything, right?" Apparently she was putting on her big sister hat right now—she'd fallen into the role seamlessly and found that she absolutely loved it. Dylan and Joe were the best brothers-in-law she could have asked for.

"Oh my God, you sound just like Mac! But yeah, I know. I'll stop." He did a little twist on the dance floor, making her laugh. "In case I haven't said it, you were a gorgeous bride. Well, you *are* a gorgeous bride. I just wanted to say officially—welcome to the family. Dylan and I are so happy to call you our sister."

She blinked back tears and waved a hand at her eyes. "Don't make me cry on my wedding day. It took Autumn forever to do my makeup."

He laughed lightly even as Dylan cut in and nudged him out of the way. Serenity grabbed Joe and pulled him into a dance and his eyes lit up.

"My brother has no rhythm." Dylan shook his head, moving to the beat. He, on the other hand, actually had some moves.

She shimmied to the beat of the music as she laughed. "You're not lying."

He snickered and said, "Congratulations again. I'm so happy for you. Both of you."

Even though they were on the dance floor, she pulled him into a big hug and squeezed so tight. "And we are so happy for you. Congratulations on getting accepted into the Corps."

His cheeks flushed slightly as he stepped back and continued dancing. "Thank you."

"Do you have any details yet?"

"Not yet. You guys will be the first to know though."

"That's enough." Mac swooped in and pulled her into his arms. "No one else gets any more dances with my bride," he practically growled. And oh, it was so sexy when he got all possessive and protective. He knew exactly how to melt her.

Laughing, she threw her arms around the neck of her new husband.

Husband!

It was wild to think the word. This gorgeous man was now her husband. Mac had a lot of layers and she was looking forward to peeling back all of them.

As he swept her into his arms for another dance, she looked around the dance floor and smiled. Bianca was there with a date, a woman she was head over heels for, and Serenity and Lucas were of course dancing with each other. Even Easton had brought a date for their wedding. All the women from her quilting class were here, and pretty much everyone who came into the grooming shop had come too. It felt like half the town was here and she loved it.

Once upon a time she'd never imagined this could be her life, that she would be surrounded with so many friends—family—but now she couldn't imagine anything else.

She looked up to find Mac watching her with those intense blue eyes, and smiled.

He leaned down slightly. "Want to get out of here and start our honeymoon early?"

"We can't do that."

"Who says? They'll be fine partying without us. We've already been here two hours. It's enough." Without waiting for a response, he scooped her up in his arms with a laugh. "Enjoy the reception," he called out.

Around them everyone laughed, but he wasn't kidding as he stalked out of the reception hall. She hadn't had a thing to drink today but felt like she'd had a few glasses of champagne. Love and happiness were a hell of a drug.

And she was brimming over with both right now, ready for this new chapter in life. She had a feeling it would be her greatest adventure.

Thank you for reading Silent Protector. If you'd like to stay in touch with Katie and be the first to learn about new releases, sign up for her newsletter at

https://katiereus.com

ACKNOWLEDGMENTS

Big thanks to everyone who helped get this book into shape! Thank you to Kaylea Cross for helping me slog through the first draft of this book. It wasn't pretty but your insight, as always, is a gift. I'm also grateful to Julia for her wonderful edits, Sarah for beta reading (and ALL the other things), and Jaycee for another gorgeous cover. And of course I'm thankful to my wonderful readers, who keep asking for more books. Thank you for taking another journey with me. To my mom, thank you for all your help in this new chapter of our lives. And I would be remiss if I didn't mention my sweet pups, who laze about day in and day out, silently supporting me.

Ancients Rising Series
Ancient Protector
Ancient Enemy
Ancient Enforcer
Ancient Vendetta
Ancient Retribution

Darkness Series
Darkness Awakened
Taste of Darkness
Beyond the Darkness
Hunted by Darkness
Into the Darkness
Saved by Darkness
Guardian of Darkness
Sentinel of Darkness
A Very Dragon Christmas
Darkness Rising

Deadly Ops Series
Targeted
Bound to Danger
Chasing Danger (novella)
Shattered Duty
Edge of Danger
A Covert Affair

Endgame Trilogy
Bishop's Knight
Bishop's Queen
Bishop's Endgame

MacArthur Family Series
Falling for Irish
Unintended Target
Saving Sienna

Moon Shifter Series
Alpha Instinct
Lover's Instinct
Primal Possession
Mating Instinct
His Untamed Desire
Avenger's Heat
Hunter Reborn
Protective Instinct
Dark Protector
A Mate for Christmas

O'Connor Family Series
Merry Christmas, Baby
Tease Me, Baby
It's Me Again, Baby
Mistletoe Me, Baby

Sin City Series (the Serafina)
First Surrender
Sensual Surrender
Sweetest Surrender
Dangerous Surrender

Verona Bay
Dark Memento
Deadly Past
Silent Protector

Linked books
Retribution
Tempting Danger

Non-series Romantic Suspense
Running From the Past
Dangerous Secrets
Killer Secrets
Deadly Obsession
Danger in Paradise
His Secret Past

Paranormal Romance
Destined Mate
Protector's Mate
A Jaguar's Kiss
Tempting the Jaguar
Enemy Mine
Heart of the Jaguar

ABOUT THE AUTHOR

Katie Reus is the *New York Times* and *USA Today* bestselling author of the Red Stone Security series, the Darkness series and the Deadly Ops series. She fell in love with romance at a young age thanks to books she pilfered from her mom's stash. Years later she loves reading romance almost as much as she loves writing it.

However, she didn't always know she wanted to be a writer. After changing majors many times, she finally graduated summa cum laude with a degree in psychology. Not long after that she discovered a new love. Writing. She now spends her days writing paranormal romance and romantic suspense. For more information on Katie please visit her website: https://katiereus.com

Made in United States
Orlando, FL
30 November 2021

10985651R00163